THE WENTWORTH TRIPLETS

MYSTERY SERIES

THE CASE OF THE CUNNING CAT

THE CASE OF THE HAIRY HIDING PLACE

JOANN KLUSMEYER

Published by Innovo Publishing, LLC
www.innovopublishing.com
1-888-546-2111

Providing Full-Service Publishing Services for Christian Authors, Artists &
Ministries: Books, eBooks, Audiobooks, Music, Screenplays, Film & Curricula

**THE WENTWORTH TRIPLETS
MYSTERY SERIES
FOR YOUNG TEENS**

VOLUME I

**THE CASE OF THE CUNNING CAT
&
THE CASE OF THE HAIRY HIDING PLACE:**
AN ANTHOLOGY OF WENTWORTH MYSTERIES

ISBN: 978-1-61314-654-5

Cover Design & Interior Layout: Innovo Publishing, LLC

Printed in the United States of America
U.S. Printing History
First Edition: 2021

Has God called you to create a Christian book, ebook, audiobook, music album,
screenplay, film, or curricula? If so, visit the ChristianPublishingPortal.com to
learn how to accomplish your calling with excellence. Learn to do everything
yourself, or hire trusted Christian Experts from our Marketplace to help.

CONTENTS

A NOTE FROM THE PUBLISHER

Although the Wentworth triplets are fictional, the models depicting them on the back cover are real triplets (Aden, Cole & Eva Claire) who, at the time, were the same age as the characters. Just like the fictional Wentworths, the real triplets and their parents are believers. And if that wasn't coincidence enough, the real dad is a world-traveling pilot just like his fictional counterpart. Interestingly, the author didn't know the models or their family. What are the odds? At Innovo we like to say, "With God—one hundred percent!"

THE CASE OF THE CUNNING CAT

D ad, I have to get my hair trimmed before we go to Africa." thirteen year old Darla stated.

"No, Dad, she looks good... if she's a porcupine," taunted Dennis, her brother.

"Or a baboon," added Danny, the other member of the Wentworth triplets.

"Or a wildebeest."

"Or a wild cat," suggested Danny, again.

"Or a...."

Darla stared from one to the other, "And your ears and noses are just fine if you are a pair of elephants, but you are not elephants. Elephants are very smart animals."

Their cousin, twelve year old Sally Copeland, measured her foot against the sole of her heavy walking boots. "Did you know that my foot is almost a half an inch longer when I stand up than when I sit down? My boots are too short for walking but just right for sitting. I don't think I need heavy walking boots for sitting."

Montgomery Wentworth, nature photographer, sat at the table with a cup of coffee and the sports page of the newspaper.

"Dad?" Darla interrupted.

"Yes, Kitten?"

"We've got to go shopping. I need a haircut and Sally's boots are too small. And, Dad, I can't find the bug cream. I think we're out."

"Then make the bugs eat their cereal with milk," Danny suggested.

"Huh?"

"If you can't find the cream, make the bugs use milk," clarified Dennis.

The girls did not answer, but turned disdainfully back to Mr. Wentworth.

"Have you ever gone up the Senegal River, Dad?"

"No, Kitten, not all the way. It's a very long river and we'll be out for at least a week, just filming the upper half of it. Documenting the lower half will take another week. We may not get all the pictures we need in a week, and if that happens, we may have to go back."

"We'll always be by the water, won't we?"

"Yes, and we'll need plenty of mosquito repellent. If we are to make the documentary film of all of the uses of the water in the Senegal River, we'll have to include the lowly mosquito with our camera."

"All of the uses?" questioned Sally. "Do you think they will all go on one film?"

"Certainly not. But we will be trying for a five-part series of one hour each segment."

"Wow! Five hours' worth!" Dennis was impressed. "That's a lot of shooting… huh?"

Dad nodded, and told Dennis, "Son, go get the mosquito nets. I seem to remember some holes in them."

"Yeah, Dad, we need new ones."

"Maybe not. Go get them."

Dennis was back with an armload of tightly woven mesh fabric.

"Look, Dad, that's where Danny got his foot caught and fell through it."

"Holes! Holes! Holes! We need five new nets," decided Danny.

"Not so fast. Do you think money grows on trees? You boys go get the repair string and tie these holes together. Make your ties tight enough to keep out the mosquitoes and that should keep you busy until the girls and I get home from shopping."

"Aw, Dad…."

"That's not fair, Dad!"

Their Dad grinned and winked at the girls. "Who said life was fair? Besides, the girls have to pack the food supply box and they won't have time to help you tie the nets." Then Dad added, "Or would you rather do the inventory of supplies and pack all the food?"

"Say, Danny, net tying isn't so bad, is it?"

"Yeah, Dad, we'll just tie."

Dad nodded his agreement, and followed the girls to the car. He noted Darla's bushy, unmanageable hair really did need help. If her mother had lived, no doubt she would know what to do with it, and in a few years, Darla herself would know. But now? What was left to do now was to have a session with the trimming shears at the barber shop.

Sally got new boots, and they bought two dozen extra thick hiking socks, interchangeable in size, for the eight assorted feet. They bought mosquito repellant, antibiotic bug cream (someone always got bitten or stung) and several rolls of very sticky fly paper (necessary for keeping insects out of the food until it could be eaten.)

By the time they got home, the boys had mended the holes in the net... most of them, anyway, and the girls began the job of food packing.

"Lots of hot chocolate envelopes. They're lightweight." Darla began. "How many? Let's see... ten days times five people, that's fifty. Then we might want extra, sometimes, so how about a hundred?"

"Well, a carton holds sixty four. How about two cartons?"

"Good. Now crackers and granola bars. Flour for biscuits but we'll have to use canned sausage and dried eggs. That takes care of breakfasts."

"No jelly?"

"I'm afraid not because the jars would be too heavy to carry. That's what Dad said. Now lunches. There's macaroni and cheese... powdered cheese, of course. Dehydrated soup and dried fruit."

Sally began to giggle and Darla joined her in hysterical laughter. "Are you remembering Danny?"

"Who ate all of that dehydrated fruit mix?"

"And then drank all that water?"

"And it started to swell up in his stomach?"

Darla sobered slightly. "But Dad got worried and thought he should go to the hospital to get Danny's stomach pumped."

"Yeah, and the closest hospital was a hundred and fifty miles away!"

"By pack train!"

"Okay, back to business. That takes care of lunches."

"Macaroni every day?"

"Well, how about the hamburger helper mixes without meat? They're light, and taste good..... anyway, they taste different from plain macaroni and cheese and it would give us a change."

"Yeah, let's put some in."

"How about tuna helper?"

"I don't know. Tuna's heavy."

"We don't need tuna. It's good without it. Mom forgot to put the tuna in the casserole one time, and we liked it just as well."

"Okay. Five of each, macaroni and cheese, hamburger helper and tuna helper. That's enough for lunches with some left over."

"Now, dinner. It's going to be heavy because we can't help it. Will there be any meat along the way?"

"Dad says don't count on it. Africa doesn't have rabbits everywhere like in the states."

"Okay. Let's start with chili and wieners. And...."

"I know what! Let's get a canned chicken and we can put dry dumplings in the broth and some extra dry milk and dry cheese. That should be good."

"I hope so."

So the supply box was packed. Cans in the bottom, lighter items on top, and envelopes of this and that were wedged around the edges of the cans. Beside the food crate, there was a case of beef jerky and the two cases of granola bars for snacks. That took care of the food.

"Sally, we forgot something."

"What?"

"Dad's coffee."

"He'll have to just get along without it. We don't have any more room."

"Do you want to tell him he'll have to do without it?"

Sally considered the problem. "I think we can find room. Here, hand me the envelopes. We can take out some of the dry onions."

"No, let's leave the onions for the soup, remember? Let's take out one of the envelopes of dry peanut butter. We're the only ones that like it, anyway. There!"

"All done. Now we can pack our own suitcases."

"It won't be cold in Africa so we won't need the insulated coveralls to sleep in, but the mosquito nets take up almost as much room. There's jeans, tee shirts, hats. The book says they are very important in Africa."

"Be sure to put in the sunburn cream."

Then they were ready. It was amazing that a whole week of life for five people could be packed into 5 suitcases, three food crates and a container for the lightweight aluminum stoves and the tiny cans of propane for them. And one more box for whatever was forgotten, and discovered at the last moment. The miscellaneous box.

The small airplane, Beechking ICU 2, waited in the airport hanger in Springfield, Misouri.

The Wentworths and Sally loaded the baggage into the van and headed north out of Branson toward Springfield. The Beechking was just a dark shape in the dim morning light when they climbed aboard, but as they arose into the sky above the mountain, the sun was already shining. It glistened off the shiny metal of the wings as they flew south, over the many lakes and ponds of the Ozark Mountains of southern Missouri.

They turned east and crossed over the mountains of eastern Missouri and the rivers reflecting silver from the rays of the morning sun.

"Where are the granola bars?" Dennis demanded.

"Oop! Darla, did you get the bars?"

"Nope! I didn't get them."

Now Danny was alert. "Somebody better have put them in or somebody is going to get tossed out in the lake."

"That's enough, kids!" came the voice from the pilot's seat.

Sally reached into the box under her seat and took out two breakfast bars. Tossing them toward the boys, she commanded, "Now shut up and get back to your checker game."

Mr. Wentworth picked up the radio mike. "Beechking ICU 2 to Memphis Tower."

"Tower to Beechking ICU 2. Go ahead."

"Beechking ICU 2 to Tower. Just passing through on schedule to Birmingham."

"Tower to Beechking ICU 2. Have a good flight."

The rolling hills and mountains stretched out beneath them. The still air, unusual for the mountains, cushioned their ride and the girls were about to doze off to sleep. The boys were not far behind, with Dennis still holding a checker in his hand.

The pilot of the small jet listened to music on his CD, stopping only to check in with the tower in Birmingham, Alabama and then Tampa, Florida. It was very late when the lights of Miami appeared below them.

"Beechking ICU 2 to Miami Tower."

"Tower to Beechking ICU 2. Go ahead."

"Request landing instructions."

"Proceed north and come in on Runway 17. Trans Atlantic is just ahead of you. You will touch down thirty seconds later, since you use less runway. Note, Cessna is immediately behind you."

"Beechking ICU 2 to Tower. Acknowledge and will comply."

Their last night in the states was spent in the jet, ready for an early start.

The blue of the ocean was below them and the blue of the sky was above. Clouds floated over the water and were not disturbed as the small jet passed through them.

The drone of the engine carrying them across the ocean made napping very easy, and the four passengers slept a lot, alternating their naps with checker games and library books. It was dusky dark as the spot of light appeared on the horizon. The spot of light became larger and brighter, and finally became a city.

The pilot announced their approach, "Beechking ICU 2 to Dakar Tower. Request permission to land."

They were now in Africa, ready to spend their first night on the continent.

The bush pilot came early with his tiny plane to take them up river to the headwaters for the beginning of the film. The little plane could land and take off where the jet could not, and was equipped with pontoons for landing on the water. It was loaded with the bulk of the supplies, and would be meeting them at various points along the way.

When the bush pilot set down on a grassy meadow at the head of the river, they were met by their guide.

"Dad, I think we messed up. I don't see a river."

Mr. Wangteya, the guide, smiled his wide, many-toothed smile. "Young ladies, be glad you see no river. Plane on the river would feed the crocodiles."

"Feed them what?"

"People. Size of her," he pointed to Sally.

"Me, too?" asked Dennis.

"Naw. You tough. Make two bites for crocodile. Chew and chew, then spit."

"Aw, Wangteya, you're just teasing."

He shook his head. "Not teasing. Come. I will toss you into Senegali to show."

"NOOOO!"

Darla had a question. "Wangteya, where did you learn to speak such good English?"

Wangteya, shook his head sadly. "School. I study, study, study." He mopped his hand across his forehead as though wiping away the sweat.

"I know what you mean," sympathized Darla. "Why did you do it if it was so hard?"

"For work. Need good speaking English to be guide to hunters of animals."

"But we're not hunters."

Wangteya nodded, "Gun or camera. Same thing. Guide shows animals and keeps hunters from getting lost. Do that and get paid."

"I see what you mean."

The first camp was set up by the pool high in the African plateau. There the water from a spring had moistened the ground and elephants had gouged with their tusks into the dirt until they had dug out a basin. The water was muddy and thick, but the long-legged birds waded at the edge, plunging their long bills into the mud. It was a perfect place to begin the film documenting the uses of the water in the African river.

"There's something using the water, Dad."

The photographer had the camera running. The large, colorful birds strolled about, peering into the thick water.

"Danny, get the little shovel."

Danny was back in a minute. "Here it is, Dad."

"Dig down right there and see if you can bring up whatever those birds are eating."

"But, Dad...."

"Start digging."

The camera clicked regularly as Danny plunged the shovel into the thick water. He brought up a scoop of slimy mud and put it on the bank. Nothing was in it. The next scoop was no better.

"Dad, I think they're eating mud."

"Keep digging."

The next shovelful of mud was deposited. With the back of the shovel, Danny spread the pile of mud thin and there was a wiggly movement in the dark mud. A chunky, fat worm wiggled out, confused at being disturbed. With the point of his shovel, Danny eased the grub out of the mud. "Get him, Dad. He was using the water."

Dad got him. The squirming, muddy grub became the star of his own film segment.

"Throw him back now, Danny."

A blue-green dragon fly darted toward the muddy bank. It settled on the mud, flexing its papery wings while it drank. Two other dragonflies joined the first, and the trio performed calisthenics with their wings. Then, all in the same instant, the three zoomed off into the African landscape.

A beautifully colored snake roped its way among the branches of a small tree, looped over one of the outer limbs and ker-plunked into the muddy water. Only its head was visible as it swam away from them.

"Bashful snake," decided Sally.

Wangteya shook his head. "Constrictor. Eats animals. You too big to eat so he will save you till he gets bigger. Then he'll be back."

"Speaking of eating, where is the food?"

They climbed back up the bluff where the bush pilot had let them out. Nothing was there. No luggage, no stove and, worst of all, no food.

"Dad!"

The photographer shook his head, sadly. "Too bad! We'll just have to live off the land."

"Aw, Dad...."

Wangteya was grinning. "Plane took gear to village. We get carriers in village to help carry bags."

Danny wondered, "How far is it to the village?" The distance between him and his next meal was of great and immediate concern.

"Three miles," was the answer.

"Oh, that's not far."

The photographer grinned. "Three miles as the crow flies, but we're not crows. Counting the ups and downs it's about seven or eight miles. So let's get started."

"How long is this river, Dad?"

"He told us it was over 1,000 miles."

"Didn't you hear him?"

"Did you think it would shrink?"

"Hush up. I'm subtracting."

"Oh, I'm glad you're not an adder."

"Adder?"

"An adder is a snake, dummy."

"I got it! After today we will have only 997 miles to go."

"Boys, save your breath for walking. We're going down over the bluff. You first, Danny. Watch for those rolling rocks. Watch where Wangteya steps."

"You next, Sally."

Sally began to crawl backward down the steep hill. Darla was close behind. Then came Dennis.

By that time Dad had his camera securely attached to his back and he followed the others down the hill.

Another tiny stream of water joined the Senegal river and the water was a little clearer now, and a little wider. Then it was gone. Entirely! The whole river had disappeared!

"Short river, huh, Dad?"

But there it was again, flowing up from among the rocks and forming a small pool. Fat little water bugs scooted around on the top of the pool on long wiry legs and tiny fish darted back and forth in the warm, shallow water.

The camera was aimed at the pool and now all the little fish will swim again each time the film is shown.

The first mile was not so bad. The second one was better but the last one was dreadful. The river had found a way to cut into a thicket of trees. Long vines hung out of the trees, and the vines had winding, sticky tendrils catching onto clothing and hair. Buzzing insects attacked their faces and arms and as the sun lowered, the mosquitoes increased. The hum of their wings was deafening. The air was black with them and they would not go away when they were shooed. A slap on the arm killed five or six, but it did not seem decrease their number.

When it seemed they could go no farther into the wet jungle, they suddenly emerged from the trees into bright sunshine and the sounds of humans and animals, and they could smell the wonderful aroma of food.

"How much farther, Wangteya?"

"More steps. Take one step then another step. We be there."

The bank of the river was low and the soft ground was hard to walk in. Water had seeped into their boots, and their arms were covered with red spots where mosquitoes had sneaked past their waving hands and attacked them. Into the jungle of vines they plunged again, ducking the hanging, clinging tendrils.

The village sounds were clearer, now, and they stepped again from the jungle of trees, vines and hanging moss, and came into a large clearing. The straw huts of the village were scattered about, each with a cooking fire beside it.

They were met by the carriers, 6 young men with shiny muscles and smiling faces, who showed them where their gear had been stowed.

"Dad, who cooks first, the girls or us?" Dany asked.

Dad took a coin form his pocket. "Heads or tails?"

"Heads."

"Tails," he pronounced. "Girls first."

Darla sniffed and looked at Sally. "Come on. We don't care. We can do it faster, anyway, and we're all hungry."

Setting up the tiny stove took only a minute. Waiting for the water to heat took a little longer.

"What shall we have? The chicken takes too long."

"Well, there's macaroni and cheese or..."

"Let's do that Mexican thing with the macaroni in it. That's pretty good, if we're hungry enough. Get two packages. Wait, get three. Wangteya might want some."

The water finally simmered and in went the spices. The smell lifted their spirits somewhat. In went the macaroni and cheese, and it smelled a little better. Finally, in went the dried tomatoes and peppers, and more spices.

From the village they saw a girl coming toward them, but she shyly hesitated before she reached them.

Sally suggested, "If we be quiet, maybe she'll come on. If we say something, we might scare her away."

Darla nodded. She smiled toward the girl, but kept stirring the food. It was getting thick and creamy. Wangteya had left them, but he might be back. Anyway, there was plenty of food.

The girl crept closer.

Sally dished up the food in their soup bowls and handed them around, and the girl came closer.

"I think she's interested in the food," Darla decided. "I'll bet she's never tasted anything like this."

Sally agreed. "We've got plenty so let's share. Be careful so we don't scare her away."

The girls took their food bowls and moved a little way toward the girl, then sat on the ground to eat. The girl came very close and stood behind Sally, looking down into her bowl. Sally held her bowl toward the girl, and she sniffed deeply. The spicy steam of the Mexican dish made her sneeze and she took several steps backward.

They began to eat and again the girl came closer. She looked in Darla's bowl. She reached her hand toward the bowl and Darla offered her another spoon. The girl dipped into the chili-mac and picked up a spoonful. She looked at it a long time, then sniffed it again. This time she didn't cough, but she made a strange face. Slowly she put the spoon in her mouth and brought it out empty. She chewed once, and her eyes popped open as though they were on springs.

Her mouth came open, too.

Darla pointed to her bowl to offer her another bite, but the girl just looked at the food. Then she turned and ran back to the village and the girls continued to eat.

After a minute the village girl was back. She touched Darla's arm and tugged at her sleeve.

"I think she wants us to go with her. Come on. Bring your dish along. Maybe she wants her mama to taste it."

The girl was motioning for them to follow her, and she stopped beside a hut where a woman was stirring something in a kettle. It was thick, dark and chunky.

The girl took Darla's spoon and dipped into the kettle, and the woman smiled at her and stopped stirring. The girl handed the spoonful of food to Darla, who sniffed it but hesitated.

"You better eat it or you'll hurt her feelings."

Darla took a bite. It was a thick, savory stew and Darla licked the spoon. The girl smiled and dipped a spoonful for Sally. The girl smiled, showing her beautiful white teeth, and she reached for their bowls.

Puzzled, they handed them to her. Without ceremony, she turned and dumped the chili mac on the ground and the woman filled their bowls with stew.

She motioned them to sit with them and eat, and they didn't need to be invited twice. The stew was delicious!

Two large dogs approached the pile of chili mac on the ground and sniffed. One walked away, but the other extended his tongue to taste it, then he sneezed and walked away, leaving the pile for the ant, who will eat anything.

It was quite dark when Darla and Sally finished their second bowl of stew. Wangteya came to the hut and picked up a bowl, and the woman filled it for him.

Oh, ho! This was Wangteya's home. It didn't take them all night to figure something out! And the girl must be his! Of course, she was!

"Wangteya, that's your daughter, isn't it?"

Wangteya nodded. "Name is Lynia."

"Lynia!"

The girl smiled and pointed to herself.

The fire burned low under the kettle and the moon was rising. The mosquitoes were becoming very insistent.

"Darla! Sally!"

"Coming, Dad." They waved to Lynia and left.

Back at the camp, water was boiling to make their evening hot chocolate. The mosquito net tents were set up around the campfire, and they sat watching the flames while sipping their drink.

"Time for evening devotions," Dad told them. "It will be the way we always do it. You think of a Bible verse you remember and tell us why you selected that one. Danny?"

"I'm thinking."

"Dennis?"

"I'm ready. 'Make a joyful noise unto the Lord.' I don't know why I thought of that one unless it's because of all the noise around me. Mosquitoes, night birds, frogs and everything, and the noise does sound a little bit joyful. At least, it might sound that way to God, since He made all of them."

At that moment, the roar of a lion was heard in the distance.

"Was that a joyful noise, Dad?"

"I don't know. If we see her tomorrow, we'll ask her."

"Her? How do you know it was a 'her'?"

"That lion is hunting and most of the hunting is done by the females, but we don't know for sure. Who's next?"

"I am," said Darla. "Mine is 'Give and it shall be given to you'. We gave Lynia a bite and she gave us a bowl full of something."

"What was it?"

"I don't know but it sure was good. We can ask Wangteya tomorrow."

"Sally?"

"I'm ready. 'The eyes of the Lord are in every place beholding the evil and the good.' I hope God's eyes are here because it seems a little spooky to me."

"Now, Danny?"

"I'm trying to remember. It's about the blessed man who is like a tree by the rivers of water. Those trees down by the river that we walked through were tough and tall so that must be the way a Christian, or the blessed man, should be."

"Very good. Mine is 'He who would have friends must show himself to be friendly.' Lynia came to us, smiling, and took the girls to her house for food. That was very friendly of her, and now we can consider her our friend. All right, into the tents you go, before the mosquitoes eat you up."

The lion roared and was answered. A bird chattered and something heavy fell to the ground near them. It was scary to think what it might be.

"Dad?"

"Yes, Danny?"

"Shouldn't we take turns keeping the fire burning?"

"Are you scared, Danny?"

"Oh, no! I just thought we might get cold."

The African sun burst forth above the trees and sent its rays down on the camp. Roosters in the village flapped their wings to crow, and from Sally's mosquito net tent came these words....

"Eighteen, nineteen, twenty, twenty one...."

From Darla's tent came, "I beat you. I have thirty one."

"I wasn't through. That was just the ones I could see."

"Ones? Ones, what?"

"What are you girls jabbering about?"

"Mosquito bites. We were just counting them. Oh, look at Danny. He looks like he has the measles!"

"I'm going to quit counting. He has me beat. I think he won the prize."

"Yeah, and I'm just ITCHING to know what the prize is," answered Danny, dryly.

"It may take us a while to decide what the prize will be, considering that we have to start from SCRATCH."

"I think I have one SPOTTED," announced Dennis, grabbing up a passing cricket. He pushed it under Danny's tent, proclaiming in a loud voice, "To Danny, for having the most mosquito bites!"

"Dad?"

"What, Kitten?"

"Why do we have mosquitoes? Surely there's a purpose. God wouldn't create something totally useless, would He?"

Dad's coffee was perking in its pot on its own little stove, and he was making his special camp biscuits. They were big, fat and heavy so no one would get hungry until lunch. He considered the problem of the mosquito. "I really can't speak for God, Kitten, but back home, the mosquitoes are eaten by the purple martin. Those birds even time their nest building and egg hatching to take advantage of the best swarms of them. Environmentalists tell us the birds can eat their weight in mosquitoes every day. Perhaps there are birds here that depend on them for food. I would guess that God considers them to be bird food, not just human annoyances."

The biscuits were in their little oven and covered the top of the stove. Dad was mixing the powdered eggs to scramble when the biscuits were done. Back in the states, they would have had bacon or sausages, but cans of meat were too heavy to bring on this safari.

"Out of bed, everyone. We have eight miles to walk before we reach the next stop, where we can meet the plane again."

"Eight miles?"

"But, Dad...?"

"Yes, but we have two days to do it in. We camp tonight where a smaller river joins the Senegal. Then the plane will take us almost to Keyes."

"Oh, boy! I can't wait to ride the barge when we go downriver from Keyes. Can we sleep on the barge, Dad?"

"Do you really want to? It would be a lot handier for the crocodiles to get at you on the barge. Personally, I plan to be in a tree."

"Me, too," decided Sally.

Dennis was thinking about something else. "Just think. The kids back in Branson have to go to school and I get to go camping."

"Yeah," agreed Danny. "Let's do this all the time, Dad. I'm going to be a photographer like you, and I don't need school."

"Now, Danny, you know the only reason you're out of school is that the trip down here must be made in October. The rainy season is almost over here and we have to come when the river still has water. In another month, the Senegal will be too low at Keyes for us to barge. You'll forget about all this fun while you're making up the lessons you missed this week."

"Aw, Dad, don't take all the fun out of it."

Danny still had his "prize" cricket, holding it by the legs, and one of the village hens came clucking toward him. He pitched the cricket toward the hen and it disappeared, instantly.

Danny announced, "I should get the next egg that hen lays. She ate my prize cricket."

Wangteya stood, restlessly, and looked down at the lounging family, so Dad decided, "Get moving with your breakfast. I see Wangteya is ready to go, and waiting on us."

There was a sudden flurry of activity and everyone was dressed, and then the bedrolls repacked in the space of three minutes.

Biscuits stuffed with scrambled eggs were stuffed into mouths. Powdered orange juice washed it down. The stoves were packed and everything was bound together with straps that were strung up on carrying poles. Then the poles were lifted to the shoulders of the "carriers." The six strong young men started jogging toward the jungle at a brisk pace.

"They hurry off to make tree camp," explained Wangteya. "We follow slow."

"I'm glad of that. I'm too full to hurry," commented Darla.

The early light was good for photographs, and the clear sparkling rays of the morning sun made the leaves of the trees shiny with sparkling dew drops. The photographer took his camera toward the river where he walked around, looking at the ground.

"Did you lose something, Dad?"

"Can we help look for it?"

"What was it?"

"A bug or beetle?"

"Thanks, kids, but I found it."

"Dad, that's just a hoof mark where a cow or something stepped in the mud," Dennis pointed out.

"Look close. It's a miniature aquarium."

Four heads bent down to look. There in the water were two tiny sticks, flipping this way and that.

"Wiggletails!" declared Sally. "I didn't know they had them in Africa!"

"Where did you think all these mosquitoes were coming from?" demanded Danny, ungraciously. "Did you think God created them individually, just for us so we wouldn't be homesick?"

"I forgot."

The photographer adjusted his lens and waited. One tiny object that looked like a bead was floating on the water. He pointed the camera and clicked. The tiny bead split open and something popped up. The bead still floated in its miniature pool. Then with a mighty effort, papery wings popped up from the bead and flexed in the morning sunshine. There was a moment's pause, then it flew away, a perfectly formed mosquito.

"Dad, that was just a mosquito," reminded Dennis.

"Why did you waste film on that thing?"

"There are hundreds of them."

"Everyone knows what they look like."

"Yeah, that was a waste of time."

"How come, Dad?"

The photographer was changing the lens of the camera and carefully putting the special one away. "Remember what we are filming, kids. We are documenting the creatures that use the water of the Senegal River and the mosquito was one of them. Wasn't it?"

"Yeah, I guess so."

"Still, I think it was just a waste of time."

"Possibly the bird who eats it wouldn't agree with you."

"Dad, look at that bird. It's after the mosquitoes. Look how it darts around."

The camera followed the bird on its swooping dives, then paused as the bird settled on a branch and began to sing.

"Let's go down to the river," suggested the guide, and the family followed. Wangteya turned for a last look at his village and he raised his hand to wave.

Darla and Sally turned just in time to see Lynia wave to her father. They waved, too, and she returned their goodbye. Too bad they hadn't had time to get to know her.

The photographer took shots of the birds along the way. White-plumed egrets strutted about on the river bank, pulling this and that up from the muddy shallows.

The spoonbills with their pink head-feathers and their rose-colored paddle-shaped bills swung their heads from side to side. How could they tell what they were getting in the muddy water? But the birds seemed to like the taste of whatever it was.

The long-legged herons waded casually around in the water, picking up crawfish and small, colorful, finned swimmers. One heron turned to look at the camera, and turned his head from side to side as if to say, "Which is my best pose?"

Wangteya led them through the twisted vines (how did the carriers manage to get the those poles loaded with luggage through here?) and the tall, tall trees.

Birds with beautifully colored beaks fluttered overhead, hooting and squeaking as toucans will.

Darla looked overhead at the toucan and said, "Look, Sally, that's the bird that advertises for the fruit flavored cereal on TV! Look at him go!"

"Hey, yeah, he's after his cereal. He must be hungry." The strong flapping wings of the toucan crashed through the tree branches as he flew away from the humans of the camera crew.

A herd of tiny deer came to drink at the river. The steenbok crept timidly toward the water, but not all of them drank at one time. Some looked around behind them, others looked at the crocodiles as they were yawning and stretching nearby. The tiny deer took turns at the water so that some of them were always watching while the others drank.

A crocodile slid soundlessly into the river, hardly making a ripple on the water, but one of the tiny deer barked with a high pitched "yip" and in an instant, nothing was visible where it had stood except tails and tiny feet, and then there was nothing at all.

The crocodile clambered back onto the sunny bank and closed his eyes. A small bird landed on his head and began to peck at his nose and around his eyes. The crocodile could have snapped up the bird matter of an instant, but it didn't. It would rather have the bugs and other creatures cleaned off its back. The huge lizard yawned widely, presenting a wavy row of sharp teeth to the camera. It closed its mouth with a snap, forcing the muddy water out of the sides and through its pointed teeth. The thick, muddy water flowed out over his lips.

Wangteya, usually silent, told them. "Must keep eyes on the croc. Sneaky and quick and can bite off a leg, like snap!" He snapped his fingers together, making a sharp sound. "You see croc, you climb tree first. Think later."

"Thanks for the warning, Wangteya. We might be tempted to think these are like the ones in the zoo... still across the fence from us."

"When do we find the hippos?" Danny asked.

Wangteya answered, "Long way to hippo. Down close to town of Keyes. Hippo needs water and Senegal gets low and river grass dies. Then the hippo has to go downstream."

"Yeah, Danny, the hippo is waiting downstream to turn our barge over, huh, Dad?"

"Very likely, Dennis."

A swarm of yellow butterflies settled on a patch of wet sand, flattening and raising their wings as they sipped moisture from the ground, and they became part of the movie.

The sun was getting hot, now, and the air around them was moist and heavy. It was a major decision as to which was worse, the mosquitoes or the sun on their heads. Some of Danny's red spots were fading, but they had been replaced with new ones.

They were walking as close as possible to the river, partly because the walking was easier, but more importantly, they might miss a good picture if they didn't.

Wangteya led the way and Sally was now following closely behind. The guide turned to speak, but at that instant, Sally saw the python slithering toward them. Nimbly, she leaped aside, just as she heard Wangteya shout, "Don't jump."

Everyone stopped mid-step as Sally landed on a bare spot of sand. The slippery sand sucked her feet up the ankles, in an instant. She stepped onto another soft spot and leaned forward on her hands to steady herself. Instantly her hands disappeared into the ground all the way up to her elbows. Her boots were sinking fast.

"Help! I'm sliding in the river!"

"I'll get you, Sally," yelled Darla, but her dad grabbed her sleeve, holding her back.

"Help me," Sally pled, already up to her ankles and elbows.

Wangteya pulled a branch from a tree and tossed it toward her. "Grab the tree!"

"I can't lift my hand," she wailed.

"Yes, you can, Sally. Get the limb, NOW!"

Sally strained to pull her right hand up from the quicksand and when she did, she plunged her left arm farther down. The quicksand sucked her under all the way up to her shoulder. She grabbed for the limb and held it, but her feet and legs were still sinking.

"Stand here," Wangteya commanded Danny, as he pointed to the end of the tree branch that lay across the stone path. "Don't move for any reason."

Danny stepped onto the end of the branch, and Wangteya disappeared into the jungle.

As Sally held to the branch and tried to pull herself up, causing the small branch began to slip, carrying Danny with it.

"DAD!"

Dad had worked his way around the quicksand to Danny's side. He stepped on the branch, adding his weight and it stopped sliding.

Sally was now in the quicksand up to her chin, with only her right arm and head showing, but here came Wangteya with a long vine. He tossed a loop of the vine toward Sally, catching her around the neck.

"Hold it," he yelled as the looped vine began to slip off, over Sally's head. Sally turned her head sideways and opened her mouth wide. She bit the vine tightly with her teeth and the vine stopped slipping.

"Good girl!"

"You hold vine," he directed Dennis. "She cannot get out alone, so we help. You wait."

They waited. Then the guide was back with a section of a fallen tree. He raised the log and let it fall into the sand beside Sally.

Carefully, he stepped onto the log and reached for her. He got a handful of her skirt collar and began to pull. The suction of the sand made her very heavy.

Her chin lifted out of the sucking sand, and he pulled some more and her shoulder was out, but then the log he stood on began to sink. Slowly but steadily the sand was sucking the log down into itself.

Wangteya leaned over and pulled on Sally's left arm, finally pulling it free. He worked her arm through the loop of the vine so that it was under her armpits.

"Let loose the branch. Hold the vine," he directed.

Sally let go of her grasp on the branch and grabbed the vine with both hands. The log Wangteya stood on had just disappeared into the sand, but at the last moment, the guide had jumped to the bank. All together they pulled, easing Sally up and out of the slippery sand. Finally she was sitting on the bank, exhausted, out of breath and pale with fright.

They dipped water from the river to rinse some of the sand of from her but her boots and clothes were full of it. When she could finally speak, she said to Wangteya, "I shouldn't have jumped, huh?"

But the guide just shrugged. "Who would know? We could pull you from the quicksand, but if you had not jumped, I could not erase the bite of the python."

"Uncle Monty, did you take a picture of the quicksand?"

"No, Sally. We won't need a picture to remember it. There are some things we will never forget, even without a picture."

"Yeah, and if your mom saw what really happened, she would never let you come with us again."

"Especially if we lost you, completely," Dennis pointed out.

"Who has the beef jerky? I'm starved," complained Danny.

"I have it," Darla said and tossed him a stick of the dried, salted beef.

"I'm sure glad it wasn't Sally who had the jerky. She would probably have dropped it and it would be gone in the quicksand."

Darla stopped suddenly, almost tripping her father.

"Dad?"

"What, Kitten?"

"Are dragons just pretend, or are they real?"

"As far as I know, they are just pretend."

"That's what I thought but, Dad, look over there."

They all looked in the direction Darla's finger pointed. Clutching a moss-covered log was a pair of scaly, long-clawed feet attached to a thick neck hanging with folds of glistening, armorlike, scaly skin. The bony-plated skull had twinkly eyes and a hard-lipped beak of a mouth. A gray-pink tongue flicked this way and that as the creature looked about.

The ugly creature eased its scaled body over the log and turned toward the water, unmindful of the whispery sound of the camera. It lowered its head into the river and swallowed twice, still looking around with its bright-button eyes.

Then it turned and walked away, leaving its claw-toed footprints in the sand, with a trail between them where its long tail had dragged.

"Just a lizard," the photographer told them. "A monitor lizard. Some people think it watches for crocodiles and clicks a warning to other animals."

"You don't think so, do you, Dad?"

"It's hard to say. I'd think more probably it clicks because of concern and mild fright, knowing it had better move away or it might get eaten. If a group of them are together, the alertness of one would warn the others." And he added, "And it would warn the crocodile as well."

In the distance they could hear excited voices. Wangteya listened for a moment.

"Carriers," he explained. "Man is injured by tiger."

"Tiger?"

"This close?"

"A man-eating tiger?"

"Is the tiger still there?"

"Did they kill it?"

"Shall we hide?"

"We could climb a tree?"

"That would be silly. Tigers climb trees better than some people do."

"What are we going to do?"

"Dad?"

"I suggest we let Wangteya finish what he was saying."

All heads turned toward the guide.

"All safe for now. Carriers throw meat so tiger is not so hungry, now."

"Meat? What kind of meat?"

"Bok. Or you say 'deer' meat."

"The tiger won't kill if it isn't hungry? Is that what you said?"

Wangteya nodded. "We think."

"I hope they fed it enough," Darla told them. "Not just an appetizer."

The voices were closer now. They stepped out of the jungle trees into a clearing with small trees and bushes scattered about. On the limbs just overhead there were several platforms made of small poles.

"Is that the bedrooms?" Darla wondered.

"I just want to find the bath tub," complained Sally. "Everything is sticking to me, and I have sand in my boots."

"Dad, we have a problem." Darla said. "Our clothes are up ahead and Sally is all wet and sandy."

"Open the suitcase and let's see what we have."

The photographer looked through the luggage and picked up a small, lightweight blanket. With a knife, he made a hole in the center. He popped it over Sally's head and it hung around her like a tent.

"There you are, Your Majesty. You have a royal robe. Take off your clothes and rinse out the sand. You can wear this while they are drying."

A small fire had been built beside the tree, and was being fed by the carriers. Small green twigs blazed and sputtered as the sap drained out onto the coals. Large pieces of meat had been speared with green limbs and they were stuck in the ground and set so they would lean over the fire. The juice from the meat dripped, smoking, into the flame, spitting and sputtering and smelling delicious.

Everyone gathered around, sniffing appreciatively, getting hungrier by the minute. The smell was so good that even the trees would be hungry if they had noses and stomachs.

"What is that meat? Jungle hares?"

"No, the pieces are too big."

"A BIG hare?"

"Look how long the leg of the animal was."

"What was it?"

"I know," decided Darla.

"What?"

"I don't want to say."

"Why?"

Sally supplied the reason. "She thinks it is those darling little steenbok deer. I do, too."

They looked at Wangteya, who nodded.

"How could you kill them? They're so cute!"

"Remember, it was the bok meat that saved the carriers from the tiger."

"Oh, yes."

"I'll eat it. I don't mind that it's cute," Danny offered. "Is it ready?"

He turned to look at his dad, who answered, "Danny, it's the boys' turn to cook. What are you going to fix for our dinner?"

Danny's eyes flew open wide. He pointed to the dripping, smoking meat.

"Dad, we...?"

"Yeah," agreed Dennis, "We want...."

"Have you been invited?"

"No, but they have so much."

The carriers were removing the meat from the sticks and placing it on wide, green leaves. With the knives they had used to cut their way through the jungle, they began to divide the meat into chunks. With fresh green sticks, they speared the great slabs of meat and distributed them to everyone, smiling broadly.

The carriers said something to Wangteya, who laughed loudly and the carriers laughed with him.

"What was funny, Dad?"

"He doesn't know. He doesn't understand them, either."

"But he could ask Wangteya."

"So could you."

"But Dad could do it better."

"Someone ask them what was funny."

"Wangteya, what was funny?"

Wangetya shook his head. He didn't want to tell them, but they insisted.

"Carriers say hurry and catch bok and cook to eat or young women would make food in the kettle that dogs did not want."

"Oh." Darla looked down at the ground.

Sally tried to defend them. "If the carriers thought our cooking was bad, they should have tasted some of the stuff Dennis and Danny cook. It's even worse."

"No, it isn't."

"Is."

"Isn't."

"That's enough, kids."

But the deer meat was a lot better than the camp-cooked macaroni, and that was agreed by all.

The carriers brought a lot of firewood into the clearing. As the sun went down, the fire was built up into a crackling mountain of flame.

Sally, huddling in her blanket robe, came close to the warmth of the fire, and they all gathered around the cheery flames.

Darla poured the cups of evening hot chocolate, and offered some to the carriers, who sniffed it and shook their heads. Dad tried to protect Darla's feelings by saying, "Maybe one has to learn to like certain flavors."

"Is it verse time yet, Dad? I have mine."

"Go ahead, Kitten."

"Mine is 'Watch and pray that you enter not into temptation'. The little steenbok had to watch and drink so they would not enter into the crocodile's mouth."

"Good. Who's next? Sally?"

"I keep thinking of when Peter was trying to walk on the water to Jesus. He started sinking and he yelled, "Lord, save me before I perish!" That's what I would have said if I had any voice."

"Aw, you got my verse!" Dennis complained. "Now I'll have to think up another one."

"I'm ready," Danny offered. "The foolish man built his house on the sand, and it washed away out from under him."

"Oh, you got the other one I just thought up! I'll have to think again," Dennis complained.

Everyone waited in silence for a few minutes.

"I've got it! I've got it! Jesus said, 'I am the vine.' That's what Wangteya tossed out to Sally."

"Very good, Dennis. Here's mine. It's in Psalms. 'You called to Me in trouble and I delivered you.' That is a promise that is good for all occasions."

"Uncle Monty?"

"Yes, Sally?"

"What makes some sand be quicksand?"

"Yeah, Dad, what?"

"That's a very good question. There are several reasons for quicksand, which just means that the sand does not pack together. Sometimes it is caused by regular, ordinary sand in a new, muddy wallow, and eventually the mud gets so much debris into it that the regular sand packs around it, and it is no longer 'quick' which is another word for 'alive'.

"Generally, though, it is a kind of sand made from certain mineral rocks that is structurally unstable and wears away easily, and the action of the water makes the grains round like marbles, instead of angular like tiny rocks. When this happens, the edges of the sand do not catch on each other, but roll around, letting anything that falls on it sink right though. If the water is full of dirt, making it muddy, the round rocks of the sand are even more slippery."

"Yeah, Uncle Monty, and every time I wiggled, I went farther down."

"That's right, and it's hard to be quiet and let someone help, because it's natural to try to get out by ourselves, and it's very scary. It's even scary for the ones on the bank."

"That's for sure."

The girls climbed up to one of the platforms stretched out on tree limbs, and zipped their sleeping bags together to make one big one.

"That way, if one of us falls out of the tree, we'll both fall!"

Dennis and Danny tied their bags to a limb, just for safety's sake, and crawled in, but their dad stood at the base of the tree, listening and watching.

Wangteya came to him. "You hear?"

The photographer nodded. "But I'm not sure what I hear."

"Probably tiger. Not full of meat."

"Has he been a big problem to the people around here?"

"I hear of him. Not many tigers here and hunting is good in the wild. Would not think of tiger coming so brave to the village. He kill a dog and a sheep, and injured a small child."

"But he hasn't actually killed a person yet?"

"Yes. Two. Young hunters from next village."

"Hmmm. After tigers gets a taste of human blood, it is hard to change them from being man-eaters."

Wangteya agreed. "Some say kill him, but government say to protect."

"How are they keeping him away from the village?"

"People throw to him meat to make him not hungry enough to kill."

"That's not good. It keeps him around."

"Right, but that is what they do. Carriers throw him bok and now he is here for more."

"Do you really think he's close?"

"Close, yes," the guide agreed. "Carriers make two fires for safer place to be. Tiger will not come between two fires... they hope."

"When we get to our luggage, I have a tranquilizer dart gun, but that will do us no good here."

"We hope for the fire," Wangteya repeated.

The dark shapes of the trees in the clearing were no longer visible in the total darkness. A sliver of pale moon was overhead and the sky was full of stars but there was no light on the banks of the Senegal except for the two crackling fires.

Three of the carriers sat on the ground and leaned against the luggage to sleep. The other three paced back and forth. When they walked beside the fires, their shadows grew into huge, grotesque shapes that were cast about into the surrounding trees.

Darla looked down at the two fires crackling hungrily at the wood. She looked around at the dark landscape and two fiery dots glistened. She rubbed her eyes and looked again. The dots were still there. She nudged Sally.

"Look over there in the dark."

"What is it? Don't try to tell me it's a rabbit."

"Sally, rabbits don't get that big."

They huddled into their sleeping bag, shivering with fright. A real, wild tiger was standing as close as next door would be if they had a door. And tigers could climb trees.

Below them by the fire, Dad, Wangteya and the three carriers were still walking around and talking low.

Sally peeked out of the sleeping bag and looked the other way. There were two more eyes.

"Look, Darla. There's another one."

"Don't tell me about it! No, wait, Sally, it's the same one. It's just moving around us."

"Dad?" Dennis whispered loudly.

"What, Son?"

"I see the tiger eyes. I can't go to sleep with him watching me."

"I know, Son, but it doesn't help to stay awake. You're just as safe if you're asleep."

"But I wish I couldn't see him."

"You can shut your eyes."

"Do we have a gun, Dad?"

"Not one big enough to kill a tiger before it got us. It would kill a snake or a small animal but not that tiger. Relax, Son, we'll be all right."

"How do you know?"

"Son, this is Wangteya's home. He's lived to be a grownup here, so he must know how to stay alive."

"That's right. I never thought of that."

Danny complained, "Hush up, Dennis. You're keeping me awake."

Darla nudged Sally, "He's back to the other side. I think he's closer, now."

"You're right."

The carriers stood close together, talking, then they talked with Wangteya. He sighed and nodded, and the young men took burning sticks from the flame and set two more fires so that the tree was surrounded by four patches of leaping flames.

"Will there be enough wood?" Mr. Wentworth wondered.

"That is a worry. We wonder about four smaller fires to be better than two big ones. We try. We have bok meat to throw, but not until we have to."

Sally shivered. "Do you hear them? They're worried. Now I'm worried."

"Dad?" Darla whispered.

"What, Kitten?"

"What time is it?"

"Almost eleven. Go to sleep if you can."

"I'll try, Dad."

"Let's count sheep, Darla," suggested Sally.

"I can't."

"Why?"

"The tiger ate up all of my sheep. Now he's after yours."

"You're right. When does it get daylight?"

"About five o'clock, I think."

"That's six hours away."

"Yeah."

The girls lay watching the stars.

"There's the dipper, the big one. Look at those three bright stars."

"Yeah. And there's the little dipper."

"Do you think the firewood will last?"

"I hope so."

The limbs of the tree swayed slightly as Dennis eased out of his sleeping bag and swung down to the ground.

"I'll help watch, Dad."

"Thanks, Son."

The activity woke up the sleeping carriers and more long dark shadows moved about the leaping flames of the fire. Always, they were watchful of the pair of shining eyes staring at them from the darkness. The fiery eyes that were circling, prowling, staring at the humans behind the fire.

Danny, trying to sleep on his platform finally sat up, rubbing his eyes.

The girls gave up sneaking peeks at the shrinking pile of wood and sat up so they could get a better look at it. It was a lot smaller, now, and it was hardly midnight.

"What time is it, Uncle Monty?"

"Ten minutes past midnight, Sally."

"Will there...?"

Her uncle answered her unspoken question. "There will be enough wood, Sally. Yes. Somehow."

Darla and Sally mentally divided the brush pile by four, for the four fires, and the piles in their minds looked very small.

Wangteya selected a stone about the size of an egg and tossed it toward the shining eyes, but they did not even blink. That was one very determined, and hungry, tiger!

Danny was awake now.

"Can we throw that leftover meat at him and make him go away?"

The guide answered, "We save the meat. We go four miles tomorrow with no fire to keep him away. Throw meat all along the way."

"Oh. I forgot about tomorrow."

"Dad?"

"Yes, Kitten?"

"We have eleven beef jerky sticks. Would they help?"

"I don't know, baby, but we'll probably try them and see. I don't know how a tiger would feel about so much salt."

Wangteya nodded. "He will eat. That hungry tiger get hungry enough to eat any American food."

"Biscuits?"

"Yes."

"Dad, we could feed him biscuits."

"There won't be enough. If he had everything we have, it wouldn't be much for a tiger."

The tree was quivering with activity on the lower platform.

"Danny, what are you doing?" complained Darla.

Danny didn't answer. Instead, he handed a pole down from the platform.

"Here, Dennis."

"What are you doing?"

"I'm taking this bed apart. We're going to need it to keep the fire going."

"Good idea," complimented Wangteya. "Tree bed had good solid wood. Save until later."

"What time is it, Dad?"

"Almost two."

"Uncle Monty, will you hand me the robe you made for me? We have to get up and take our bed apart."

Wangteya examined the poles being handed out of the tree. He selected six of the biggest. "Save six," he told them. "We put fire on the end to make fire club when we start to walk. Carriers will hold fire club. Our hunters know how to do this."

The photographer nodded. "Good idea. I can carry a club, too."

"No," said Wangteya. "You need hands for the pictures. It was the agreement. You pay us to protect. We protect."

So it was settled.

"What time is it, Dad?"

"Twenty minutes after three."

"Dad?"

"Yes, Kitten?"

"I wonder why God bothered to make evil tigers."

"I'm sure He had His reasons. For one thing, the tiger is a scavenger who helps cull out the sick and old animals."

"But he eats them up!"

"If he didn't, they would starve to death, slowly and painfully."

"But, Dad, we aren't sick and old and he's after us."

"You're right. This is unusual behavior for a jungle tiger. Ordinarily, he would be more interested in hunting animals than people. We don't know why he is so intent on stalking people."

He unpacked the small, snake-killing gun and fired it into the air. The shining dots staring from the darkness, did not blink. This tiger was not afraid of the gun, so the photographer put it away.

"What time is it, Dad?"

"Three twenty-five."

"We have three more poles for each fire in addition to the six we're saving."

"Does it get daylight by five?"

"No, more like five thirty."

"Let's see. That would be one and one half poles per hour. Not enough."

Wangteya stepped outside the circle of flame and the fiery eyes turned to look at him. No one breathed. A low rumbling vibration of a growl could be heard above the snap and crackle of the fire. Wangteya came back to the tree behind the fires.

"What time is it, Dad?"

"Almost four."

"They're putting on the last of the wood. We're going to run out, aren't we, Dad?"

"No, the coals will last a while. We need more light before we start out."

The shining eyes were closer to the ground, now, showing that the tiger was lying down. Waiting… Watching….

"I'm scared. Maybe we should sing some songs," suggested Sally.

Dennis agreed. "Yeah, why don't you and Darla sing? That'll drive him away if anything will."

Sally turned to stare at her cousin. "Why don't you step out there so he can get a good look at you. He'd run off crying."

"Not as quick as if you girls started to sing."

Wangteya placed the last of the poles so their small end would be in the fire to catch a flame, ready to become the fire clubs the carriers would use.

"What time is it, Dad?"

"Five o'clock. Time to start breakfast."

"Breakfast?"

"Are we going to wait to eat?"

Dad set up the stove and put the oven on it. "We must wait until near daylight, anyway, so we may as well eat breakfast. It will give us something to do."

The huge, savory biscuits arose in their pan, brown, fragrant and heavy. They were broken open to be stuffed with scrambled eggs, made from the powder. Even the carriers were glad to have something to do and ate biscuits with the family. They would undoubtedly have preferred meat, but that must be saved for the tiger. They ate all the biscuits they could hold and that would have to be enough to last through the last four miles of jungle to the waiting bush pilot.

The birds overhead began to whistle and chatter and the monkeys started to bark as daylight came. The sky became lighter, then the yellow rays of the sun shone through the trees.

The tiger had moved back a little as daylight came, but now he sat bravely in plain sight, watching the activity. The dying fire was no longer a protection and the tiger was very alert as though planning his method and time of attack.

The bundles and bags were strung up on the carrying poles and lifted to the strong shoulders of the carriers, and the blazing fire clubs were put in their hands.

Wangteya directed the spacing.

"Camera man goes first beside first carrier so he see what to take pictures of. Young women go behind him, like so. Then carrier, and then young men will follows. Next carrier here, and I will be in back. Tiger will follow for a while."

"Then what?" Dennis asked.

Wangteya looked puzzled, but Danny clarified the question.

"When the tiger quits following, then what will happen?"

Wangteya sighed. "Tall bluff to climb, then tiger will want to spring out and down to catch someone."

"Where will you be then?"

"Everywhere."

The remaining meat was divided into four small parcels, each one tied with a rope and threaded over the carrier's poles.

It was now light enough to keep from stepping on snakes, so they started out. The tiger followed slowly behind, creeping from tree to bush. Just before they entered the jungle, the first packet of meat was flung back toward him. With a savage growl, he tore into the meat, snarling and hissing.

Quickly the safari disappeared into the thick growth of trees. Overhead the tall trees extended, some a hundred feet tall and their limbs intertwined. Birds fluttered around and monkeys swung, chattering, from the limbs.

The carriers with the fire clubs chopped away vines with their sharp knives, and picked careful paths around the quicksand by the river. Behind them was the tiger, his stripes often visible between the trees. Each time they looked around, he seemed to be closer.

Wangteya tossed the tiger the second bag of bones. "No more until we reach the bluff," he told the huge cat.

The photographer filmed the birds and the monkeys and he had many pictures of the tiger, creeping along in the trees behind them.

A hedgehog waddled out of the bushes, heading for the river bank to drink. Her fat babies waddled behind her and they did not know that they became movie stars as they lapped the river water. The tiger ignored the hedgehog and continued to follow the safari. There was a reason. The little hedgehogs were covered with sharp quills.

The fire in the clubs had burned low and they were now useless as protection, so they were tossed into the river and the water hissed out the fire. Just ahead of them was the bluff on which the bush pilot waited.

Wangteya told them to stop and rest. "To be ready," he explained. "We climb the bluff at one time. No rest. Tiger likes to be on top. He wants to look down and when we climb, he jumps down. We use all eyes to be careful."

He spoke plainly and firmly, looking at each person.

"Is there a question?" he asked.

Dennis had one. "Where is he now? I don't see him?"

"I don't know about him, but I know he knows about us."

"But he's not back there."

Wangteya shook his head. "I like the tiger I see better than the one I do not see who could be in the tree over my head."

Five sets of eyes looked up, half expecting to see the yellow and black stripes of the tiger overhead on a limb.

"We start," commanded the guide. "Carriers on the bluff hold down the climbing rope. Young men go first up the bluff and young ladies come to climb in front of me. Now!"

The carriers were first, hoisting the luggage from ledge to ledge, sometimes looping a rope over a tree limb or root to help them. The boys scrambled up behind the carriers, sharing the rope, and the girls followed closely behind them.

Wangteya and the photographer came last, hoping to see exactly where the tiger was, but he was still hidden. Either that, or he had a plan!

When the boys were near the top of the bluff, the guide called to them, "New plan. Young men wait on ledge, and pass the young women by you. Carriers ready to help pull up over the edge."

Sally passed by the boys and reached the grassy meadow at the top of the bluff. Darla held to the rope the carriers offered, and scrambled up to join her. Parts of the bluff caved away beneath their feet, sending clods and stones down onto the rest of the safari.

Danny was next at the rope. The stone holding the rope over the ledge loosened and shifted, jerking Danny away from the edge of the bluff. A tree limb struck him in the face and he grabbed it, kicking his feet for a solid limb. Amid the shuffle of waving branches, he found footing. The climbing rope now hung down toward Dennis.

Dennis was waiting his turn, but Danny was still in the tree. Should he move the rope to Danny, or climb it while he could? He looked down toward his father and the guide working their way up, and there between him and them was the tiger, stretched out across a limb of a tree just below Danny's feet.

"DAD! TIGER!"

The men looked up just in time to see the crouch of the tiger preparing to spring.

The photographer pointed the small gun at the treetops and fired, causing the tiger to lower himself to the limb once more and the men scrambled back down the bluff.

The tiger, seeing his chance, followed them. Wangteya tossed the two remaining meat bundles toward the big cat. His growls and snarls could be heard all the way to the top of the bluff as the guide and the photographer clawed their way from rock to ledge to low hanging limb.

Dennis hesitated no longer, but shinnied hand over hand like a monkey up to the top of the rope, and was pulled over the lip of the bluff by the carriers, who then swung the rope toward Danny. Making the rope fall through the limbs without catching on them took some skill, but when Danny could reach the rope, he was at the top in minutes. Amid the falling dirt and rocks, the two men finally pulled themselves over the grassy ledge.

Everyone was on the top, now, and the village could be seen in the near distance. The carriers set off on a jogging pace and the rest of the party ran to keep up with them.

Huffing and panting, they entered the cluster of grass-topped mud huts. The bush pilot's plane was waiting, and while Wangteya warned the villagers of the tiger, the photographer rummaged though his gear for the tranquilizing dart gun. It might take a little while for the tiger to work his way up the bluff, but he was sure to follow them into the village. The tranquilizer would buy them some time to consider the problem.

The villagers huddled together in groups, shouldering their weapons and shooing small children into the huts, which would offer no protection should the tiger wish to attack. Every pair of eyes was trained toward the bluff as the huge cat approached...slowly... tiredly... toward them. Why would anything so fierce as a tiger walk so slowly? But he did!

Through the powerful binoculars, the photographer watched the progress of the yellow and black striped animal.

"He's limping on his left front paw. He must have an injury."

As the tiger crept closer, it hid, crouching, behind a cluster of bushes. They waited, but they did not see any black and yellow emerge from its hiding place.

"Wangteya, come with me, will you? I want to get a little closer."

Stealthily, they approached the tiger, the photographer keeping it in his camera sights. The beast watched the men, warning them with its rumbling, vibrating growl.

The photographer paused, knelt to take aim, then fired the dart toward the cat's shoulder. It was a sure shot. The cat flinched slightly and lashed its tail from side to side. Finally, he lowered his chin to his paws and closed his eyes, then rolled gently over to his side.

Wangteya quickly tied the tiger's feet together with a strong rope. Dennis was first to reach the site, with Danny close behind, then came the girls.

The tiger looked peacefully asleep, seeming like a big kitten, just taking a nap in the sun.

The photographer felt the bones of the tiger's legs, then examined the huge paws.

"Look what I found," he told them as he separated the toes of the tiger's front paw. The toe pads were red and infected from a cut, seemingly made by the aluminum ring from the top of a soft drink can. Apparently, when the tiger had pounced, landing on his front feet, his toes had spread and the metal ring slipped between. Then when he raised his foot, the ring cut into the flesh, wedging itself firmly into the thick toe pads where the tiger could not dislodge it with his teeth. From the look of the paw, the metal ring had been lodged between his toes for a long time.

The tiger slept on while the metal soda tab was removed, and the infected flesh trimmed away. Wangteya brought medicinal leaves to wipe into the wound, cleansing it.

"Kitten, go get the bug cream. It is an antibiotic which should help clear up this infection."

Darla ran to get it, and the tiger was beginning to try to open his eyes. He stared wildly at the humans so close to him, but the paralyzing drug would not let him move.

The frightened beast tried to struggle away as the cream was spread on his sore, red toes. He now had a small movement in his feet, but the rope held his legs tightly together.

"What now?" Danny asked. "You have to let him loose, don't you, Dad?"

"Yes, but first we have to decide where to take him. I have an idea the poor beast's foot was too painful to hunt, and that is why he attacked the villages. We need to get him back into the jungle."

"Carry him?"

"Drug him?"

"Scare him?"

"Airlift him?"

Their dad nodded. "You guessed it."

"Airlift him?"

"In the airplane?"

"With us?"

"Does the pilot know?"

"I'll bet he won't let you do it."

"He's too big to get through the door."

"Tie him to the wing."

"Tie him under the plane."

"Make him a swing."

Their dad nodded again. "You guessed it."

"Make him a swing?"

"Yeah! Make him a rope swing so he can hang down under the plane."

"And we find a place, and drop him off."

"What do you mean 'we'? Notice the size of that plane. That tiger will be a load all by himself."

"Does the pilot know?"

"Dad, I'll bet you have to do the flying."

"Dad, he's growling."

"Get more rope, Danny. Dennis, go ask the pilot to come out here."

It took another dart but the tiger was finally bound securely.

The pilot taxied the plane to the tiger and watched as the photographer and the guide secured the beast to the belly of his tiny plane. Across the meadow runway he rolled with the sleeping cat, and the photographer and the bush pilot soared off the bluff and away over the trees into the jungle.

"I'm hungry," complained Darla.

"What's for dinner?" asked Sally.

Danny and Dennis looked at each other, shrugged, then headed toward the village.

"Do you think they have something good to eat cooking in one of those huts?" Danny wondered.

"We could ask," agreed Dennis.

"You better not," warned Darla.

"We can make macaroni and cheese," decided Dennis. "That's easy. Come on, Dan..."

The girls looked at each other, and Sally wrinkled her nose. "I don't want macaroni, do you, Darla?"

"No. I want chicken dumplings."

"Then make dinner yourself," suggested Danny.

"All right, but you get the water and find the can opener."

"It's a deal."

Darla opened the tall can of boned chicken while Sally set out the onion flakes, dry milk and powdered cheese. The tiny stove finally had the water simmering, so Sally tossed in the chicken and the onion flakes and turned the fire low. Some things just naturally had to be cooked slowly, and chicken dumplings was one of those things.

Between activities, they kept turning their eyes to the bluff searching for the tiny airplane to return, while Wangteya sat on the ground and napped, leaning against a tree trunk.

Darla dropped the dried dumplings into the simmering broth while Sally slowly stirred the chicken pieces with the long-handled spoon. Dumplings were good because they soaked up the rich chicken flavor while they cooked, and that made them very fat and tender and full of flavor. One little package of dumplings turned into a big kettle full of food.

When the dumplings were all in the broth, the lid was returned to the kettle and the fire was turned very low, to keep them hot until their dad and the pilot returned. Then they all ran to the edge of the bluff to watch, as though if they concentrated on it, Dad would be back sooner.

A tiny dark dot appeared in the sky over the jungle, steadily growing larger. Next, the dot was the size of a small bird, then a huge eagle, and finally it became a small plane that set itself down at the edge of the bluff and taxied toward the village.

The girls filled the soup bowls, and the pilot sniffed appreciatively, so a bowl was filled for him. Then Wangteya became interested and the carriers, who had not had a chance to hunt for meat, gathered around.

A good thing about dumplings was that there was always enough.

The carriers said some words in their language and Wangteya interpreted. "They say young women are getting better with the cooking. Even some dogs would like this food."

That was not much of a compliment, but it would have to do. That, and the fact that everyone wanted seconds.

The sun had hardly set when the weariness of the day set in, and it was decided it was time for bed. The tiger who had kept them awake last night would not bother them tonight. Over their bedtime hot chocolate, everyone tried to remember a Bible verse that would describe something that happened this eventful day.

"I can't, Dad. My brain is already asleep," Dennis decided.

"Wake it up, then," Dad commanded. "We had a lot of interesting things happen today."

There was a long silence.

"Darla?"

"I'm not ready. I want to think of a really good one."

"Sally?"

"I'm thinking. I don't exactly remember how it goes, but it is about God giving us strength to run without getting tired. We were up all night, and then we had to scramble to get up the bluff away from the tiger, but we made it."

"Good. Danny?"

"I keep thinking of the one about a living dog being better than a dead lion, because a dead animal would not have any strength at all. Dad, the tiger would have died if we hadn't been here, wouldn't it?"

"Likely it would have, because the villagers had no tranquilizing dart so they could not get close enough to help it, and they would have finally had to kill it to save their own lives."

"But, Dad," Danny continued, "why would the Bible talk about live dogs and dead lions?"

"There could be several reasons, Son, but the one I like would be that though we may not be able to do something great, there is always something we can do. If we don't have the strength of a lion, perhaps we have the speed of a dog. Dennis?"

"My brain is still asleep."

"DANNY! LOOK AT THAT TIGER BEHIND DENNIS!"

Dennis jumped up and turned around. "Where? Where?"

"Now, Dennis, your brain is awake and you can remember a verse."

"The only one I can think of is about David saying God was his shepherd, and let him lay down in the green pastures, so he could restore his soul. Here we are on a green meadow, and I'm ready to lie down."

"Dad, he uses that one all the time!"

Dad nodded. "Perhaps it is one he understands best. Now, Darla?"

"Mine is ' Faith without works is dead.' God said He would take care of us, but if we had not built the fire and stayed behind it, the tiger would have killed us. We have to have faith that God will take care of us, but also we must do what we can."

"Very good. Mine is 'God loveth a cheerful giver.' The dinner cooks were happy to give out their food even though some people had said some unpleasant things about their cooking."

"Yeah, Dad," agreed Darla. "I thought about that one, too, but I thought it would be impolite for me to say it, since Sally and I were the cooks."

Dennis was already asleep in his bedroll, and the others were not far behind.

The moon was high and bright, and the jungle noise was a symphony all around them, when Dennis loudly whispered, "DAD!"

"What, Dennis?"

"There's something in my bedroll!"

"Besides you?"

"Yeah, and it's squirming."

"DON'T MOVE!" his dad commanded sharply. "Danny, wake up and help me."

Danny sat up rubbing his eyes. "What, Dad?"

"Danny, hold the foot of Dennis' sleeping bag. I'm going to pull him out, very quickly."

Danny leaned over and held to the foot of the bag while his dad took Dennis' arms. Quickly slipping him out of the bedroll, he patted the fabric until he found the lump. He worked the lump to the head of the bag and a small black snake appeared. The reptile uncoiled itself and crawled sluggishly away.

"A snake!" Dennis said, disgustedly. "That's what I thought it was."

"Right, and it could have been a poisonous one. This is the last time we are going to be so careless. No matter how sleepy we are, we have to fasten that mosquito net to the ground over us. That little snake probably thought you were a soft, warm rock."

"Then he couldn't have touched Dennis' head."

"Huh?"

"Because then he would have thought he was a HARD warm rock."

"Go to sleep, boys."

They didn't need a second command, and the morning sun caught them still asleep. It was the heat on the warm sleeping bags that finally aroused them. The bush pilot was packed and ready to go, but he was willing to be persuaded to wait around for hot breakfast biscuits.

Wangteya was going on with them down the river, but the carriers would now return to their village. All the bundles could be transported by airplane hop from here to Keyes. From here on, each nightly camp was close to a flat clearing where the bush pilot could bring down the plane.

"Dad, I want to send a gift back to Lynia, but I don't have anything she would like. I wish I had some jewelry or something I could give her to remember us by."

"What about something to eat? That's what she gave you."

"Aw, Dad, her food is a lot better than ours."

"I know what, Darla," Sally offered. "Granola bars!"

"Granola bars? Do you really think she would like them?"

"Let's ask her daddy."

Wangteya sampled the chocolate-covered bar of cereal and toasted nuts and nodded. "Lynia would like. She would give half to her mama."

"Then we will send two bars. You tell the carriers to take it to her?"

The bars left camp with the six carriers as they jogged away. They turned back toward the village and the trees swallowed them into its leafy jungle path.

Next on the list of camera subjects was the hippopotamus. The river was a lot wider now, making the current swift, and it would become much deeper as other small streams joined it.

The camera caught the river birds as they drank or fished in the shallow water on the edge of the river. The zebra came to drink, and stood in a nervous herd, drinking in shifts, some watching while others lowered their heads to the water.

Elephants came plodding to the bank of the Senegal and waded into the river. They spouted streams of water into the air and trumpeted their noisy call. Baby elephants rolled and splashed around their mother's feet, playing and happy in their daily bath. Then everyone took a bath in the drinking water, and then they took a final drink in their bath water!

The airplane took them to their next overnight camp farther down the river, where they made their last night camp on this part of the Senegal. The river was so swollen it could sustain barge traffic, and the activity was great. It did not, however, seem to disturb the hippos.

That night, camp would be on the ground beside the airplane, and they could rest well, because if a tiger came, which was not likely, they could just jump into the plane. They awoke early to the splash of the hippos in the water.

The name of the hippos meant 'water horse', so naturally they would be in the water a lot. That also meant a lot of filming would have to be done underwater.

"Dad, Dennis and I could take the pictures, couldn't we?"

"You can take some of them, but only from inside the decoy. Those animals are very big, and, though they are grass eaters, and are not interested in tasting you, they could kill you and not know it. Go ahead and put the decoy together, and get started. We'll see how it goes."

The decoy was a huge plastic hippopotamus, made to be snapped together in the center. The 'skin' of the hippo had many transparent places, which were actually camera lenses, for many different shots. There was plenty of room inside the body for oxygen tanks, more underwater cameras and two people. Inside the decoy, they could approach fairly close to the live animals without fear, although pulley ropes were attached to the plastic skin of the decoy so it could be pulled from the water quickly, if it should become necessary for the photographers to escape danger.

"I'll take the front of the hippo," Dennis announced.

"All right," agreed Danny. "I don't mind the back."

"Hey, wait! Who said it would be you two that would get to wear the hippo into the water?"

"Well, we...."

"We didn't think you girls would want to."

"Whoa, there, kids. We can all take a turn. In a situation like this, it's just about impossible to take too many pictures.

The fake hippo was snapped together and his stretchy middle was put in place. Dennis crawled up through the hole in its stomach and stepped into the front legs. They were so far apart that it was hard for him to stand. After much huffing and puffing, Danny was in the back legs.

"Let's walk," came Dennis' muffled voice.

"All right."

The plastic fake hippo shuddered, squirmed and fell over on its side.

"You pushed it over," accused Dennis.

"No, I didn't. I just took a step with my right foot."

"You should have started with your left because I started with my right, and that made two feet from the same side in the air at the same time. No wonder it fell over."

"How did I know? I can't see your feet."

"That's enough, boys. Now get back in there and get started together."

"All right, Dad."

The baby hippo was lifted upright and the boys crawled back into its hollow interior.

"Left, right, left, right," and the legs began to move. The beast began to shuffle noisily toward the river. At the edge of the water, the hippo turned its head toward the photographer.

"Dad?"

"What now, Dennis?"

"Do crocs eat hippos?"

"No, hippos eat crocs... or at least, they've been seen to bite them. Crocs never attack hippos."

"Good."

The animal began to waddle forward again. Then it stopped.

"Dad?"

"Yes, Dennis?"

"I don't want to eat a crocodile."

Then from the rear of the hippo came another voice. "Dennis, if you don't start moving and quit stopping, I'm going to bite you myself. Guess where!"

"Okay! Okay! I'm going."

Deeper into the water went the hippo. A voice from the bank yelled, "BOYS! Don't go too close. Stay as far away from the live animals as you can, and still get the pictures."

The rear of the hippo answered, "Sure, Dad."

Then the little hippo was under water. A few bubbles came to the top, then nothing more was seen of the animal.

The small hippo walked along the muddy bottom of the Senegal River directly toward the live hippos. One of the beasts turned to look at him, then continued feeding on the grasses growing up through the water. Another adult hippo took one step toward the 'baby'.

The rear of the baby reached up to the front and began to pull back on the front half. The front half's hands felt around in the water for the hands of the rear half, and pushed them away.

The front half kept walking, and the rear half could do nothing but follow.

Another large animal took a step closer. Now five large adults were looking at the baby. Then all of the animals began to come closer.

The front of the 'baby' made a sudden turn toward the bank, causing the whole animal to flip over. It struggled for a minute, finally succeeding in getting back on its feet. Then the adult animals began to back away, still staring at the strange baby.

Just at that moment, both the front and rear of the animal released a lung-full of oxygen at the same time, causing bubbles to rise up in a stream from the 'baby's' stomach, waist, mouth and tail. The horrified adults turned, suddenly, and galloped off, their feet hardly touching the mud on the river bottom.

The 'baby' began to waddle to the shore. It pulled itself up, dripping, from the water and rolled over. The rear half complained, "Dad, he was going to go over to the real ones, and you told him not to."

"I wasn't either."

"Yes, you were."

"That's enough, boys. Climb out."

Darla watched her brothers crawl out of the plastic hippo and complained, "Look, Dad, they scared everybody off. You should have let us go first."

Thoughtfully, her dad looked at Darla and her cousin. "Are you sure you want to go out there in this?"

"We sure do."

"All right. Get going. Take pictures of whatever you can see."

"I want the back," announced Sally, " so I can pinch you and make you come back if I get scared."

The baby hippo waddled back into the water.

"I'm glad hippos bite crocs instead of the other way around," commented the rear end.

"Me, too, but we won't get that close to one."

"Girls, don't you go far."

The little hippo answered, "We won't, Dad."

It was a different world as seen from the inside of the hippo. The water that looked muddy and dark from the surface only looked dull green from below. Green water plants grew in clusters. Tiny brown fish hid within their schools, and darted from clump to clump of the grass. A jiggle of the grass clump sent them zipping off to another hiding place.

A small snake swam by, its head held high up out of the water. From below, it appeared to be a rope hanging down from the ceiling, rippling its body. The hippo took a few more steps and released oxygen. Bubbles arose in streams.

The front of the hippo stepped on a submerged log, laying on the bottom of the river. The back half followed.

Then the 'log' stood up on its short legs and began to move. The end of it turned and a huge eye opened. The front of the 'log' split open and rows of large, sharp teeth appeared. With one mighty flip of its tail, the 'log' pushed out from under the feet of the 'hippo', knocking it over. The 'log' scooted away and into the deep water.

All of a sudden, a girl popped up out of the tummy of the little hippo and swam to the surface, dog paddling furiously toward the bank. Seconds later another girl broke through the water and followed.

The little hippo, now much lighter, floated gracefully to the surface of the river and hovered there, its nose, ears and back end showing above the water.

It bobbed along on the water toward the live hippos. One real hippo came close to the baby and touched noses with it. The 'baby' bobbed up and down with pleasure, and also because of the water movement around the huge adult. The large hippo wiggled its ears at the baby but the little one's plastic ears did not respond.

The adult touched noses again, continuing to wiggle its ears, but the baby still did nothing. The adult yawned a very bored yawn and turned away. Apparently the baby did not wish to talk.

The current of the river began to turn the baby around. It bumped against the adult and the larger animal wheeled around suddenly and bumped against the hollow baby, sending it skidding across the water toward the photographer. The light plastic baby bounced along on the current, finally bumping against the bank where its owners stood.

"Hooray!"

"Bravo!"

"Smart baby!"

"The baby knew how to take pictures without us!"

The photographer hauled the baby up the bank and called to Dennis. "Get in the back, Son, we're going in again."

Once more the baby hippo waddled into the water. In less than fifteen minutes, it came back, struggling up the muddy bank amid the cheers of the spectators on the bank.

"I can't wait to see the pictures," yelled Sally.

"Me, either, but we'll have to wait till we get home, won't we, Dad? You'll have to send it off when we're in Keyes tomorrow, won't you?"

"Dad?"

"Yes, Danny?"

"You remember you promised to put together a film to show in biology class at school?"

Dennis added, "Yeah, and if it's good enough, maybe we won't have make up work in that class. Can you make it really good, Dad?"

"Boys, I thought all of our films were good. Tell me how you would like this one to be."

"Oh, boy! Let's plan it now."

"First we'd have to have that big puddle of muddy water where the elephants gouged out the dirt with their tusks. That was right up there at the beginning, where the river was just a trickle."

"Then we wouldn't want to leave out the mosquitoes. Let's put in a picture of Dennis and his cricket prize!"

"No. The kids at school get to see enough of him. They wouldn't appreciate all his spots."

"Well, there's all the birds. Everyone likes pictures of birds. We have them wading, fishing, flying and just looking at us. That will take up a lot of film. Maybe we can't get them all in the film."

"Yeah, because we'll need space for the steenbok and the monitor lizard. And that herd of zebra were so pretty. Especially the babies, the way they looked like little striped ponies."

"Dad, when you took pictures of the tiger eyes in the dark, did you use the low light film so maybe we can see part of the tiger's face, at least some of the stripes?"

"Sure he did. Dad always uses the right film."

"Well, I hope it looks scary enough."

"I know he got a picture of the tiger on the limb, ready to pounce down on him... didn't you, Dad? That might be the scariest shot of all."

"I know he got a lot of footage of the tiger limping toward us, and of its sore foot. I don't want those pictures in the school film. It might take away from the scariness."

"I wish we had a few shots of Lynia. She was so pretty and had such a nice smile."

"Did you get some, Dad?"

"You did? Oh, goodie! I think she should go in the picture. She used the water from the river, I'm sure. Maybe she took a bath there. Anyway, she ate animals that used the water, like the deer meat stew."

"What was next? The hippos? That will be fun! Put in all the footage, like where the girls bailed out, right there in the river. That should bring a laugh."

"How about when you and Danny tipped over, before you even got in the water? How about that for a laugh?"

"Dad, did you shoot the part where the baby hippo stepped on the submerged log that opened its mouth, and swam away?"

"You did? Good!"

"Dad, did you take pictures of the tiger after you let her out in the jungle?"

"Of course he did. He takes pictures of everything."

"If you did, Dad, I changed my mind and I want it in the school film. I don't think it would take away from the scariness. A wounded tiger is just as dangerous, and maybe more so, if she gets hungry enough."

"I wonder how that metal pop top got way down here in the middle of Africa?"

"Out of someone's camping gear, I'll bet."

"Dad, this is the halfway point, isn't it? Well, let's make one school film for the first half, and another from the rest of the river. If we had two films, that would surely get us out of biology make-up classes."

The photographer looked from one to the other of the four chattering kids.

"All right, kids. I have a deal to make with you. My job is to make the documentary our customer ordered. If you are wanting to get out of make-up class, then it should be you who cuts and edits the film for school."

"Aw, Dad, you do it so much faster. I don't...."

"There's no use arguing with Dad. He doesn't change his mind. Let's make a list of what we want in it."

"I'd rather go watch the tugs bring up the barges. I just can't wait to get to ride on them."

"Yeah, let's plan later. I hear tug whistles. Let's hurry!"

"Yeah, man! The film can wait till we get home."

"Race you!"

THE CASE OF THE HAIRY HIDING PLACE

The small jet airplane circled the sky over the airport in Adelaide, Australia. Four noses were pressed to the windows of the airplane and four pairs of eyes searched the ground below.

"I don't see any," complained thirteen-year-old Dennis as he peered out the window.

"Any what?" wondered Danny, his thirteen-year-old brother.

"Kangaroos," answered Dennis. "Anything that can jump thirty feet in one jump should be visible from the air."

"In downtown Adelaide?" scorned Darla. "They don't let kangaroos come into the town." Darla was the third member of the Wentworth triplets.

"How could they keep them out of town if they wanted to hop in?" argued Dennis. "If I could jump thirty feet in one jump, I'd go anywhere I wanted to go."

"They don't all jump that far. It's just the big ones that jump thirty feet,' advised Sally, the triplet's twelve-year-old cousin. "It says in the book that most of them jump fifteen to twenty two feet. Besides, what would a kangaroo want in town? They eat grass."

"But what if the kangaroo didn't read the book? Then he wouldn't know that he probably couldn't jump thirty feet," insisted Dennis.

"Oh, hush! And besides that, those littler ones are not kangaroos. They're wallabies." pointed out Danny.

"Then they aren't kangaroos," Dennis argued.

"Yes, they are."

"No, they're not. If they're wallabies, then they aren't kangaroos."

"But listen to the book," Sally insisted. "It says there are some that are only nine inches high. Wouldn't that be cute?"

"But they can't jump thirty feet."

"I wish I had one," Darla told them.

"One what?"

"Nine inch Kangaroo. I'd keep him in the back yard to play with."

"But you know we can't have pets in the mobile home park," reminded Danny.

Then Sally butted in. "Your mobile home park isn't the only place in Branson, Missouri. If Darla had a nine inch kangaroo, he could stay in my back yard."

"No, he couldn't."

"Why not?"

"Because Aunt Eloise wouldn't let him, that's why."

"She might."

"No, she wouldn't. She'd say it looked like a big rat to her, and you know how she feels about rats. Remember Dad telling about scaring her with mice and rats when they were kids?"

"But a kangaroo isn't a rat, and I'd just explain that to her. I'll bet she would agree when she saw how cute it was."

"She wouldn't."

"She might."

"But she wouldn't."

From the cockpit of the plane, a stern voice advised. "All right, kids. Shut up and buckle your seat belts. We're going down." Then he picked up his microphone.

"Beechking ICU 2 to Adelaide Tower. Come in?"

"Adelaide Tower to Beechking ICU 2. Go ahead."

"Beechking to Tower. Request landing instructions."

The voice with the interesting accent advised in a crackle of static, "Tower to Beechking. Go north and come in on runway three as indicated by the lights. Welcome to Australia."

The houses of Adelaide, Australia became clearer and streets and cars could now be seen. Then, just ahead, there was the stretch of runway assigned to the Beechking jet piloted by Montgomery

Wentworth, nature photographer, and his three children and one niece.

The small jet touched down and taxied to the Adelaide Tower. The passengers transferred themselves and their gear to the rented helicopter for the next leg of the expedition. Mr. Wentworth would be photographing Australia's "pocketed animals" for a nature film company located in Kansas City, Missouri. He would be creating a film comparing the Australian marsupials, the "pocketed animals," with their counterpart animals in other countries.

The family had arranged to stay in a lineman shanty house, which belonged to a huge sheep ranch. It had been built for use of ranch employees who took care of the distant herds of sheep. The Australian sheep ranch was so large that, even by pickup truck, the distant parts of it would be too far to travel to each day. Small cabins were spaced all about the landscape for use of those working in the area.

The cabin where the Wentworths would stay was called East Slope Three, and was located near a working mine. Gemstones called opals were taken from the rock where they had been formed and were shipped away to decorate jewelry all over the world.

"Dad, I want to get an opal from that mine." Darla shouted above the roar of the helicopter engine.

Dad said nothing because Danny butted in, "Yeah, I'll bet you do. You and fifty million other people. Opals are valuable, you know. They don't just hand them out like suckers in the doctor's office."

"All I want is a little chip. I think they only get valuable if they're big and if they get polished up and set in gold or silver."

"Would you like to bet on that? Black opals are valuable no matter what size they are."

"Is that right, Dad?"

"You don't need to ask Dad," Danny insisted. "I read all about opals and I know what the book said."

"So what makes them black?"

"Well, they…."

"So what makes them black, if you know so much?" repeated Dennis.

Danny hesitated.

"You don't know, do you? I thought you said you knew everything."

"Sure I know what makes them black."

"What?"

"They have something in them that makes them black."

"See, you don't know."

"Coal is black," offered Sally. "But it's diamonds that are composed similar to coal, not opals."

"Carbon makes coal black. Maybe that's what makes opals black, too."

"Does Australia have carbon in its soil?"

"Yeah. Uncle Monty, does Australia have carbon in its soil?"

"Yes, Sally. Parts of Australia have a lot of carbon and you're right that carbon can color other minerals, even opals. Carbon and other dark minerals can seep through the water and stain layers of silica mineral that forms opals. It can create the pattern we think is attractive, and that's what makes an opal valuable."

"See," bragged Danny. "I was right. Dad said it was black stuff that caused the color and I was right."

"Yeah, I guess, but I still want a piece of opal. Dad, do you think we might get to go down into the mine? Like a tour, or something?"

"I don't know, Kitten. But I suspect we can ask about it. Right now we're looking for a number '3,' so we'll know we've reached East Slope Three. Everyone help me look."

"But, Dad...."

"Yes, Dennis?"

"We're too high to see house numbers, and I don't even see a house. All I can see is land and more land. It looks a lot like west Texas or New Mexico."

"Keep looking, Dennis."

For a few minutes the helicopter motor roared and the blade clap-clapped as five pairs of eyes searched the landscape below.

"Hey, Uncle Monty?"

"Yes, Sally?"

"I see something. See those white lines? They almost look like a huge '3' that has been painted on the ground. See it, way over there?"

"I see it, too," Dennis yelled. "What a funny place for a house number."

"Perhaps not so funny if the only way you get there is from the air, as we're doing." Mr. Wentworth pointed out. "Many people in

Australia use small airplanes and helicopters, almost more than cars and trucks, and when you look down on them, all rooftops look alike. This ranch has all of its outposts numbered so a person can be sure of being at the right place before putting down on the ground."

The huge number '3' became even larger as the helicopter neared it. They lowered to a short landing strip beside a tiny, grass roofed cabin.

"Oh, look at the darling house! It looks like it belongs in old English storybooks," Darla decided. "I've never seen a thatch roof. I always thought they would leak when it rained."

"Well, Kitten, that's not much of a worry here. It really doesn't rain very much," her father explained. "However, thatch roofs are surprisingly effective, even in rainy climates. There is a correct way to lay the grass so that the water will follow the rooflines all the way to the eaves and not soak through into the houses."

The chopper swung around the huge '3' and set down on the tiny runway. They could see the cabin better, now, with no trees in the way. One tall eucalyptus tree grew very close to the little house, creating a dense shade over part of the roof.

"Look at those trees! Aren't they the ones that… oh, look! There it is! A koala bear!" squealed Darla.

"Where?"

"Right up there by that big limb. That is one, isn't it?"

"Yeah, Dad, look up there. A koala bear!"

"You're right, kids, except that it is a koala marsupial, not a koala bear."

"But, Dad, they call them bears.'

"True, but they're wrong when they do."

"They look like bears."

"I know why they're not bears," decided Danny. "They all have baby pockets and real bears don't have them."

"Right, but that's not the only difference. Bears have adapted their diet and range so that if one food is not available, they can eat something else. The koala eats only eucalyptus leaves. Also, if there is a forest fire or certain other dangers, the bear can run before it, and possibly escape. The poor, dumb koala can only wait and watch until the fire kills him. Actually, forest fires are one of the biggest enemies of koala."

"I want to climb up that tree to him, Uncle Monty. Will he bite, do you think?"

"No, Sally, but wait a while about that climb. We will want to take some close up pictures of him, and we don't want to disturb any of the animals unnecessarily."

"Can I take the picture?" Sally asked. "I've never taken any real pictures that you could use."

"I don't know why not, Sally. But first we have to get settled in. Everyone grab a load and bring it on in. Danny and Dennis, you boys team up on the food chest and come on."

The tiny cabin had a kitchen/dining room/living room combination and one tiny bedroom on the first floor. A ladder went from the downstairs through a hole in the ceiling to an attic room overhead. There, up under the thatch roof, was a small bedroom with two low beds at one end. The grass roof came together in a peak overhead. It was like standing in a triangle. Absolutely charming!

Darla called to her father through the ladder opening. "We want the upstairs, Dad. All right?"

Dennis and Danny came through the door carrying the heavy food chest. "I want the upstairs, Dad." Dennis requested.

"But you haven't even seen it."

"No, but I want it."

"Oh, you're just being mean."

"No." Dennis insisted. "I have just as much right as you. It wasn't my fault I didn't get in the house first."

"Dad, he's just being hateful."

Dennis grinned at Darla. "I'll trade you something, though."

"Trade what?"

"First turn at cooking dinner. You cook, you can have the upstairs."

"But it's boy's turn. That's what Dad said."

"It wouldn't be boy's turn if you'd trade."

"But...."

"Then I want the upstairs room."

"Oh, all right. We don't care, do we, Sally?"

Sally didn't answer. She was busy spreading her sleeping bag over one of the narrow beds. "Look, Darla, this is going to be fun. Spread your bedroll over that bed and let's see how it looks."

"Sally, we've got to go cook."

"I know, but spread out your bedroll first. It won't take but a minute. See? Doesn't that look nice? I wish I had a room like this at home."

"Me, too. We'll come back up here just as soon as we finish with dinner. Let's go fix it now."

They descended the ladder and looked into the food box.

"Where shall we start?"

"Well, here's tuna. We could make that thing we made while we camped in the mountains. You know, with onions and eggs. And we could have scalloped potatoes with it. Here's the scalloped potato mix. See, there's lots of it."

The two tiny aluminum stoves were fitted with their propane cans and they had water boiling in no time. Into the kettle went the potatoes to be stirred carefully. The thick sauce of the scalloped potato mix was very bad about scorching if it was not stirred every minute. When the potatoes were thick and creamy, they were set aside and Dad's coffee pot was set on that stove.

The other stove had been heating the heavy iron skillet to brown the onions. When the onions were brown and fragrant, Sally stirred while Darla broke six eggs into the skillet and turned down the flame. Eggs got rubbery if the fire was too hot. Three cans of tuna were dumped into the skillet and left on the fire just long enough to get warm all the way through.

"Come and get it, everybody! Dinner's ready!"

The Australian night came quickly. Long before they had thoroughly investigated the cabin, darkness had settled around them. The koalas became just black lumps in the trees, then they disappeared completely. The giant trees were grouped around the little cabin as though to protect it from the world. One tree was so close that the animals could have stepped onto the thatch roof of the cabin if they had wanted to.

"Sally, let's go up and see if we can see the koala through the upstairs window."

They raced up the ladder as Mr. Wentworth sat at the tiny dining table, examining the camera equipment, cleaning lenses and sorting out the various kinds of equipment. Dennis and Danny were unpacking their bedrolls and trying to decide where to put them.

From the upstairs window, the girls leaned out to see if the koalas were close. When they looked up, there was nothing. The darkness had completely hidden them.

There was, however, something to be seen out on the horizon. A tiny light was visible as it filtered through the limbs of the eucalyptus tree.

"Look, someone's coming."

"I wonder who."

They watched for a minute but the light did not move.

"Look, it's in the exact same place. Hey, I know what it is. Remember where the opal mine is?"

"Yeah, and that must be the night light."

"To keep thieves away, maybe?"

"Why not? Opals are very valuable and there must be people who want to steal them."

"Probably...."

A voice came up from below. "Girls, time for evening devotion. Come on down."

The water for the bedtime hot chocolate was simmering on the stove. The envelopes containing the mix had been opened and dumped into the thick mugs. Dennis poured the water into the cups, filling the cabin with fragrant steam. Danny passed the cups around.

Dad began, "Who's ready to quote a Bible verse and tell us why you chose that particular verse."

Darla drew in a breath, but hesitated. Then, "I wanted a verse about windows but all I could think of was Noah making a window in the ark. That's not really the kind of verse I had in mind."

Sally butted in, "Oh, there's one about God making windows in heaven to pour down blessings. I don't know just how it goes but I think it's in the Old Testament. If I had my Bible, I could find it. I want to take some pictures out of our little window upstairs. I wonder if God looks out His window at us? If He has a camera, I'll bet He could get some really good scenes from way up where He is. But I guess there are a lot of things happening on earth that He would not want to remember, huh?"

"I suspect you're right, Sally. Are you ready, Dennis?"

"I remember a proverb by King Solomon that says, 'Rejoice not when thine enemy falleth.' It's like when a person wins an argument he shouldn't say, 'Ha, ha, I'm smarter than you because I won the argument.' And, Dad, I have no idea why I thought of that one."

"That's all right, Dennis. Now Danny."

"I thought of a verse that says, 'Come before His presence with singing and into His courts with praise.' That probably means God likes everyone's voice, even if they can't sing very well. Like those big black birds outside."

Dennis added, "God should like everyone's voice. He made them."

"That's right," their father answered. "And mine is, 'He will give thee the uttermost parts of the earth for a possession.' Our family is more fortunate than a lot of people because we actually get to see and enjoy some of those uttermost parts of the earth. But then, many others get to enjoy them through the pictures we take. Now, off to bed with you, and girls, don't you be talking and giggling instead of sleeping. Get your rest; we have a lot to do tomorrow."

In no time, it seemed, it was morning. The Australian sun was instant and dazzling as it spread across the plains. Five pairs of eyes were suddenly wide open and ready for the day.

Mr. Wentworth made the breakfast, as he always did. He baked his fat, fragrant biscuits in a tiny oven set on one of the miniature stoves. The family sat around the table and ate, making sandwiches of biscuits, butter and jam. The kids sipped orange juice while their dad had coffee.

"What do we film first, Dad?" Danny asked.

"Can I take some pictures, Uncle Monty?"

"Are we going to take pictures of that marsupial mole? We don't have a camera little enough to get into a hole, do we?"

"You mean we're going to forget about it?"

"Ah, we can't do that! I'd really like to see one. Where are they?"

"In the ground."

"Dad…?"

"Yes, Kitten?"

"Where is that opal mine? Sally and I saw a light from the upstairs window and we thought it might be from the mine."

"That's possible," agreed her dad.

"Well, if it was the mine, it is very close. I really want to go over there."

"Yeah, Uncle Monty. We really want to take a tour of the mine."

"We can't." decided Danny. "We have to go film the wombat."

"Dad, let's do the kangaroos first."

"No, Dad said the wombats."

"We have to find one before we can film him."

"Film her. The females have the pockets."

"How do we find one? They hide in the daytime, don't they?"

"Yeah, and I know why."

"So do I. The light hurts their eyes."

"No. It's because they're embarrassed by their stupid name."

"Wombat? No, that's not why."

"I know why. It's because they're nocturnal and have to sleep during the day."

"I knew that."

"But, Dad, how are we going to find them?"

"Dad…?

"Yes, Dennis?"

"If they're asleep in their burrows, how can we take pictures of them?"

"That's a good question," his dad said. "We'll just have to locate an animal and work it out from there. We know they eat grass roots and all kinds of plants so we'll look for a grassy place where they could have made a burrow."

"Will it take all day?"

"Yes, Kitten, I think it probably will. Be sure to put some water and some beef jerky in the chopper. We might get a bit hungry before we get home. It's boy's turn to cook dinner, so you fellows decide now what we're going to have. We won't want to be wasting time when we come home hungry."

"We'll be fast, Dad. We're going to have crackers and chili beans."

"And peaches."

"Aw, Dad, they always do that."

"We always do what?"

"You always pick the easy things to cook."

Danny grinned. "Don't worry. Next time we'll cook you up a mess of koala burgers."

"Yuck!" commented Darla, but Sally stared at them and pointed out, "You do and the Australian Government will lock you up and throw away the key. Wouldn't they, Uncle Monty?"

"They'd have to catch me first," teased Danny.

After breakfast they scrambled aboard the helicopter. The clap-clap-clap sound of the chopper blades spread out over the Australian plains but it was ignored by the herds of sheep grazing on the sparse grass of the pastures. The sheep moved slowly along, grazing steadily as though they were accustomed to noisy machinery passing overhead. From high in the air, the sheep looked like tan cotton balls.

"Look at those sheep down there. There must be a million of them."

"Of course there's sheep down there. This is a sheep ranch."

Then, like grains of popcorn which were just starting to pop, some of the cotton balls seemed to explode into the air and bounce about.

"Look, Dad! There's the kangaroo!"

"That's right, Danny. Get the camera. This is a shot we really want to get. Someone else get the other camera. I'm going to circle and come in as low as I can without scaring the animals."

Danny hurried the camera out of its case and aimed, waiting for the jumping animals to come into focus. Darla grabbed the other one and adjusted for wide angle and began shooting. The chopper circled wide and came back toward the kangaroos.

The sheep grazed on and did not seem a bit frightened of the helicopter. Noisy aircraft was just another happening of the day to them. The kangaroos did not seem particularly frightened, either, and nibbled grass with the sheep, continuing to bounce about. The helicopter did not come really close, but the camera would take care of that. The close-up lens would bring the strange animals up close enough to count their whiskers.

In less than an hour of shooting, the aircraft was on its way and five pairs of eyes sought for a likely looking grassy ditch, or, as was locally known, a dry billabong.

Ah, there was one, just below them. The pilot set the chopper down in the shallow ditch.

"Now, fan out and look for a hole in the dirt bank."

"How big?"

"About the size of a soccer ball."

They spread out in five directions, eyes glued to the ground, paying close attention to small bushes and clumps of grass. Where would a wombat be?

"I found a hole," called Sally. "Actually, I found two holes."

Everyone came running. There were two holes about ten feet apart.

"How can we tell if one is in there?"

"We dig. Dennis, go get the little shovels. And bring the cameras, and we'll take some pictures before we disturb the burrows."

The photographer handed the shovels to the girls. "Here, girls, scoop some of that dirt away so we can see which way the burrow goes. Be careful not to poke your shovel into an animal."

"Do they bite?"

"No, we don't think so, but go slowly, anyway. You boys keep looking out for more holes. This may be a very good place for them to come if they're social, like American prairie dogs. I think we may find several dens along this bank."

Sally scooped out another shovel full of dirt. "Look, Uncle Monty, the burrow goes straight back. How far shall I dig?"

"A little farther but go carefully. Just pretend you're remodeling his house for him. We don't want all of the roof to cave in."

The photographer tapped gently on the ground leading away from the entrance of the wombat burrow, then carefully lifted a shovel full of dirt, revealing a cross section of the inside of the tunnel. He lowered the camera gently into the burrow. There was always the possibility, just by chance, that he would get a picture of the occupant and builder of the tunnel. If not, he would get a good picture of the shape of an empty tunnel. He was just taking up the camera when Danny yelled.

"Hey, Dad, hurry and come here. I caught one."

"Stay back, Danny."

"I am, Dad. I'm standing way back. It's Dennis that has a hold on it."

"DENNIS!"

"It's all right, Dad. It doesn't mind being held. It must be tame because it isn't even trying to get away."

Dad came hurrying up with the camera. " Now let him loose, Dennis and get out of the way."

Before Dennis could obey, his father changed the command.

"No, wait, Dennis. The animal doesn't seem to be disturbed at all. Just lay it over on its side, Son. I want to zoom in on the pocket. This could be our best shot of the pouch."

Dennis eased the unresisting animal over on its side, and it began to struggle weakly, trying to get away. Dennis pushed firmly on the animal and it gave up the struggle and remained still. A fur ball slid away from it and rolled to the ground.

Under the amazed eyes of the family, the fur ball sprouted feet and a nose and became a baby wombat. The mother raised her head to look about for the baby, but the small one just stared wonderingly about.

The mother finally saw her baby and attempted to struggle to her feet. Dennis released his grasp and the mother took a wobble step toward the baby and nudged it with her nose.

"Why is she so tame, Dad?"

"Son, I don't know, but I don't think she's really tame. I think it might be possible that she's sick."

"Sick?"

"She could have gotten into some poison somewhere. That would be my best guess."

"Poison? Why would poison be laying around where she could get it?"

"There is a chance the poison was not meant for her."

"But why, Dad?"

"Yeah, why would someone want to poison her and her baby?"

"Farmers, most likely," came the answer. "This land out here seems to be a long way from any farm, but wombat burrows do a lot of harm to the farmer's crops and grain fields. Also, their abandoned burrows make a home for rabbits, and rabbits do even greater damage to the crops than the wombats. The burrows make a safe place for the rabbits to hide from their natural predators, then they over-breed."

"But to poison them…."

"I know, Son, but years ago in the old American west, ranchers tried to poison the wolves and coyotes because they raided the sheep and cattle. The poison killed a lot of them, but it didn't help a great deal. The deer, the elk and the moose that the wolves were eating, as well as some cattle, became overpopulated. They ate up their grass on the mountains and came down in the valleys and ate grass the ranchers intended for their cows. So killing the wolves didn't really help, if it meant there was not enough grass.

"When there are too many of one kind of animal, they eat up the food supply faster than it can grow back. Then some go hungry and die. A lot of the others are not as strong as they should be. It would seem that being killed instantly by a predator would be better than a slow death of starvation and disease. We must be careful and long-sighted about tampering with mother nature."

Darla had been studying the animal while her father talked.

"Dad, I know what's wrong with that wombat."

"What, Darla?"

"Remember when Dennis turned her over? Well, I remember that her baby pocket was on backward. Could that make her sick?

"Huh?"

"Her baby pocket. Didn't you notice it was on upside down? Instead of opening on the side toward her head, opened toward her tail. She couldn't even see into her pocket to see if her baby was there."

"Yeah, and he fell out when she turned over," put in Sally.

Danny thought for a minute. "Yeah, Dad, it was. I remember it was on backward."

"Shall I turn her over again?" asked Dennis. "Than you can see for sure."

"No, Dennis. We took a lot of pictures and we can look at them later. To answer your question, Darla, the pocket was not on backward. Remember these are animals that push through the dirt, crawling along on their stomachs. They shove the dirt beneath them and push it behind. If they had pockets like kangaroos, they might push dirt into the pocket, accidentally, while they were digging. So her pocket was not on wrong, and she does appear to have gotten some poison, but maybe not enough to kill her. We're going to go away and leave her alone. She's had enough misery without us standing around talking."

"Dad?"

"Yes, Kitten?"

Darla hesitated, staring down at the animal. "How could anything be so ugly as a mama wombat? The baby is kind of cute, but that mama has not one pretty thing about her."

"You're right, when you talk about the way we see her. It's like saying beauty is in the eye of the beholder. I think that mama may appear to be very beautiful to the baby, and he might think you're the ugliest thing he's ever seen. So let's go and leave them alone."

"What now, Dad?"

"It's rather early but I believe we'll go back to the cabin for a while and return to this spot later on in the evening. We might be lucky enough to capture a good shot or two of the animals coming and going to their burrows."

"Dad, what I really want is to see that opal mine. Do you think we could stop and ask the owner if we could look inside? He might not care."

Mr. Wentworth thought a minute. "I suppose we could. We really do have a little extra time right now."

The helicopter arose from the grassy ditch and circled around. Back over the grazing sheep it whirred and over the bouncing kangaroos that grazed with the sheep.

The chopper settled down on the runway near the entrance of the opal mine. A lot of four wheeled carts were setting about, and there were a number of pieces of heavy digging machinery and a lot of steel poles. Behind the mine was a group of huts used by the native laborers. All in all it was a very simple, unimpressive place. All of the activity of the mine was underground.

Mr. Wentworth walked to the entrance of the mine and was met by a large man wearing coveralls. They talked for a minute, then the large man motioned the four young people to join them.

Dad introduced them. "Mr. Longley, these are my kids who want to see what you have underground. Kids, this is Mr. Longley, who is the manager of this mine. He has offered to show us around."

"Oh, boy!"

"Can we take pictures?"

"No, Darla," Mr. Wentworth told her hastily. "We mustn't expect to be allowed to photograph the mine."

But Mr. Longley chuckled and assured them. "Little lady, you take all the pictures you want to take. You might even send one or two to me if you think of it."

"Oh, goodie! Wait till I go back and get a camera."

They entered the dim doorway to the interior of the mine. Lights, actually just bare electric bulbs, hung down from the ceiling here and there throughout the cavern. A long hall, perhaps more like a tunnel, slanted down into the ground.

The farther the tunnel extended, the lower it went into the earth. Huge rocks had been chipped out of the walls and been brought up to the surface. Piles of smaller rocks lay around, waiting to be hauled up.

"Where are all the opals, Mr. Longley?"

The mine manager chuckled. "That's exactly the question I ask every day, young man. If I just knew where they were, I wouldn't have to spend so much time looking for them where they aren't."

"But you do find some, don't you?"

"Yes, we find a lot of them. Some are very valuable and a lot of others are not worth very much. We take all we get, however, and ship them away to be made into jewelry and many other decorative items."

"How do you get them out of here?" Danny asked.

Dennis answered, "With a drill and a pick, huh?"

But Danny insisted, "I mean out of Australia. How do you get the opals away from here. I don't see any trucks going by."

"Oh, that's simple. We pack them, number them, and wait for the mail plane to take them away."

"Mail plane?"

Mr. Longley explained, "Once a week the mail comes to us by small plane. It lands on the airstrip over there by East Slope Three, near where you're staying."

"You know about us?"

"Oh, yes, to be sure. The ranch owner explained that you would be here for a few days. If he hadn't told us in advance, we would have been on the radio reporting you to mine security before your chopper ever landed. We keep a very tight security here because the size of the gem stones makes them very easy to steal."

"People steal from you?"

"Yes, I'm sorry to say. People do steal. Opals, like diamonds and gold, are so small and they can be picked up and carried out, even by our own workers. Of course, to be worth anything, they have to be sold somewhere. Most of our workers have no place to sell them, so they're not even tempted. They would rather have the bonus we pay for finding really a good piece."

"Hmmmmm, I never thought about that."

"Yes, and it ends up that we have everyone watching everyone else, and we give a reward when someone is spotted trying to get away with anything. Actually, we do rather well most of the time, but sometimes we have our troubles. It happens in all mines."

A rumbly wagon full of rock chips came by them, drowning out the sound of his voice. When he could speak again, he pointed to a colored strip on the wall by shining his flashlight on it.

"Look over here at this interesting mineral deposit," he pointed out. "See how it follows the line of the rock?"

"Is that an opal? It doesn't really look like I thought it would."

"It isn't an opal. It is just an accumulation of minerals in sandstone but that is the way opals are made. The minerals seep into low areas and become pooled up on rock ledges. The moisture slowly drains away, leaving an accumulation in pockets like this. After a million years of constant pressure, this is what you see. Then you might even find a vein of real opal."

"But not always?"

He shook his head. "No, not always, but sometimes we get very lucky. Young lady, aim your camera over here."

Darla came with the camera. "Is that an opal?"

"Yes, that is opal."

"Why don't you take it out of the ground?"

"We will, but first we have to remove a lot of rock."

Sally reached out and touched the rough material. "Do you ever have opals that you throw away?" she asked.

"Yeah," chimed in Darla, "Like tiny, little pieces?"

Mr. Longley chuckled. "Oh, my, no! We keep every little scrap. Even the very tiny pieces have their value."

"Oh," responded Darla.

Mr. Longley stroked his chin. "But now, if I'm not mistaken, you ladies were hoping for a little souvenir of your trip through a real mine? A little something to show to the girls back at school?"

"Well, we…." Darla tried to be polite.

"So come on along and let me show you some of the rocks we do throw away. Really, I think some of them are as pretty as some of the opal we keep, but they do not cut and polish well, and they are not what we call valuable stones, so they can only be thrown out."

"Where?" Sally demanded eagerly.

"Can we go see them now?"

"Yes, we could, ladies, but wouldn't you rather continue the tour? Or are you tired of listening to me talk?"

"Oh, we'll finish the tour," they all agreed.

There were men here and there who were chipping, drilling, shoveling debris and scraping. They were intent on carefully teasing the stone away from the gem deposit, working in the dim light of the cavern. On their heads, they wore little caps with a light attached to it. The light shone in the direction they turned their heads. One man stood somewhat apart, watching the other men. He did not do any work, only kept his eye on the other miners.

Mr. Longley introduced the man. "This is my security foreman, Jungili. He is in charge of the gems after they are mined until they are shipped away on the mail plane. He makes certain none are lost either accidentally or through theft."

The foreman nodded to them, unsmilingly, and he said nothing.

"What else does a foreman do?" Dennis wondered.

"In our mine the foreman also takes care of problems, listening to the miners when they have complaints, and he watches visitors and any other persons who are in their area. The foreman has a very important job, and I could never get along without the foremen. I can't be everywhere and I must have someone I can trust."

"But do you have much trouble with thieves?" Dennis probed.

"Well, Son, it's hard to tell, in a mine. If the thief is so clever that you never see him steal, then how could you know if he did it?"

"I see what you mean."

"But there is one thing that is in our favor. A thief is never satisfied. If they would be content to steal one or two small gems, then they would probably never be caught. But they get greedy. If they figure out how they can steal one or two, they want to steal a lot more. Then they have to find an illegal source to dispose of the stones, and they have to take a great number of them to make it worthwhile for the 'fence' to take the risk of selling them. It gets rather complicated, and that's why we need a good foreman with eyes in the back of his head, so to speak."

The tour was over, and Mr. Longley led them to the scrap pile. These rocks were those the miners mucked away from the gem stones, and scooped into carts to be hauled away to the surface. The broken chunks of rock were dumped outside the mine entrance in a huge pile.

The rock pile contained chips of gray and black and some had deposits of color on one side. Some had shades of blue and red, and some were white streaked with dark gray.

"Are all these 'throw-away' stones?" Darla asked, unbelievingly.

"All of them. Take any you like."

"Oh, boy! Look at these, Sally. Let's take a lot of them."

But their father reminded her, "Girls, remember that we came in a small airplane. Don't get so many that the plane won't take off."

"Aw, Dad...."

"I know what," Sally decided. "We brought in a heavy food box but we'll be eating all that up. So we could take out the same weight as the food we brought in."

"Good thinking," complimented her uncle.

Even the boys became interested, and bent down to examine the rocks in the pile.

"Look here, Darla, this is a really pretty one."

"Oh, it is! Look at this one, Sally! Hey, Dad, why would they throw away something this pretty?"

"I don't know, Kitten. I am really not up on the value of opals, and I wouldn't know a valuable one if I saw it. Remember that Mr. Longley told us a lot of really pretty stones were thrown away."

"I found one" Dennis yelled. "And here's some more. Come and look!"

"How many?"

"Oh, maybe seven or eight. No, here's another one!"

Sally and Darla ran to look at the rocks. "You know, I've never seen many opals, but I think if these were polished up and set in gold or silver, they would look exactly like I remember."

"Then let's do it. I still have my rock tumbler," agreed Sally.

"We can try, girls, but I think you mustn't get your hopes up. Mr. Longley said these rocks were different from the opals and if they were any good, they wouldn't be out here."

"Yeah, well, anyway they're really nice."

"I have two more," Danny called out. "How many do you have, Den?"

"Let's see. That makes fourteen in all. That makes seven for Darla and seven for Sally. Look, Dad!"

"Yes, they're pretty and now we have to be going so we'll be ready to be back to that ditch to watch for the wombats. Into the chopper, everyone."

As they climbed into the helicopter, the native foreman, Jungili, watched them. Mr. Wentworth waved to him but he did not respond. He just stared in the direction of the helicopter.

"Is Jungili an aborigine, Dad?"

"I would suspect so, from his name and his darker skin. However, it's hard to tell. The natives have mixed with the Europeans who invaded the land over the years, so, like in America, one can't always be sure who is who."

Dennis nodded, "A lot of the miners looked like him. I wish we knew what their names are. I've never heard of a name like Jungili before. Were the aborigines the original Australians? Like the American Indians were the original Americans?"

"Yes, they are," his father told him, "and I suspect the unusual names come from their original language."

"I wonder if those men really like working down there in that dark mine?"

"At least it's cool down there."

"It's probably considered a good job."

"I wonder how much money they make?"

"Yeah, and there aren't even any stores close. Where do they spend their money?"

"Maybe if they earn a lot of money, they can move to town."

"But then they wouldn't have a job."

"I wonder if they have families that live with them in those little huts."

"Now that it's too late, I can think of a lot of questions to ask Mr. Longley."

The noisy chopper landed on the airstrip beside East Slope Three.

"Get a move on, boys, and get dinner heated up. We need to get on back to the wombats and I really want to catch them on film as they leave their burrows."

"Dad?"

"Yes, Kitten?"

"Can Sally and I stay here at the cabin while you and the boys go take the pictures?"

"No, Darla, I need you to go with me."

"But Dad, we wanted to play with that koala."

"You heard me. I need all hands on the cameras. We'll all be busy because the area has a number of holes and I don't want to miss anything at any of them. You really have to go this time, but you can make friends with the koala later."

After a meal of chili beans with crackers, along with canned peaches, they were on their way again. Cameras and lights were tucked away in the aircraft.

As they flew over the herd of grazing sheep they saw a truck parked among the animals. A man was moving some sheep toward the truck, and seemed to be loading some of them aboard.

"Where would they be taking those sheep, Dad? See, he's got six of them cut out of the flock." Danny squinted as he stared down at the backs of the animals.

Dennis cut in, "Maybe they're sick and he's taking them to the vet."

"Sheep don't get sick, do they?"

"Sure they get sick. Everything gets sick sometime. How far away is the vet, I wonder?"

"Son, the people who herd sheep out here would have to have their own vet in camp. It would not be possible to run a truck into Adelaide or somewhere else every time an animal wasn't feeling well."

"But those sheep aren't sick."

"How can you tell from way up here?"

"Because I can see. Look, one of them rammed that man in the backside and almost knocked him down. He doesn't look sick to me."

"Then where would they be going?"

"Maybe he sold them."

"Just six of them? That doesn't make sense."

"Maybe he's going to butcher them."

"Maybe…."

"There he goes! He finally got one of them in the truck."

"Dennis, are you taking a picture of those sheep?"

"Yeah, neat! I got a shot of that sheep butting the man. That'll be funny."

It was about two hours later that all the pictures of the wombats were taken. The obliging animals wandered out of their burrows for a night of hunting and whatever else it is that wombats do, and many hours of film now waited in the cameras. The ugly, slow-moving animals would never know that they were now movie stars. The chopper hovered over the flat Australian countryside, over the opal mine, and then circled back toward East Slope Three.

"Look, that truck is still down there with those sheep. He got six of them in it."

"I told you he would."

"And he's too late to get anywhere to a vet tonight. See, he's stopping over there at the mine."

"Look, someone is going out to the truck to talk."

"I'm hungry."

"Me, too. I want a granola bar with my bedtime chocolate."

"I think that truck driver must be a friend of Mr. Jungili, because they're standing there talking."

"Hey, I got a picture of Mr. Jungili. I know that's him because the close-up lens shows how he's losing his hair on top."

"Are you wasting space in that camera?"

"No, Dad said it was hard to waste any exposure. Pictures that don't seem important now can become important later."

"Even of Mr. Jungili?"

"Why not?"

"Maybe."

Later that evening as they were sipping chocolate, Sally volunteered, "I have my verse ready. 'The Lord loveth a cheerful giver.' Mr. Longley was certainly cheerful when he gave us those pretty rocks. I'm sure the Lord must love him."

"And I'm ready," Darla announced. "It's a verse in Malachi about God making up His valuable jewels and when He did, He would remember to include people who fear Him and listen to what He says.

I think probably He considers Christians to be beautiful enough to be part of a crown, and He means that they are His jewels."

"Very good. Now Dennis."

"I got it. 'Judge not that ye be not judged.' I don't know why I thought of that one unless it was because we were trying to figure out why that man would be loading those sheep so late in the day. It really wasn't any of our business why he was doing that."

"Fine. Danny?"

"Yeah. 'Be not overcome of evil but overcome evil with good.' That would mean we have to have more good than bad, or else the bad will take over. Isn't that right?"

"Well, Son, if you are referring to good and bad habits, you are right. Of course, if you are talking about sin, only God can remove sin and we have to have His constant help to stay away from sin. We pray that we will not be led into temptation. Very good, Danny."

Then he added, "Mine is, 'Man looketh on the outward appearance but God looketh on the heart.' That reminds us that God sees things we don't see. We don't know why people act and feel the way they do, but God does. He knows everything about us, so it pays to trust Him completely. Now off to bed with you. Tomorrow will be a busy day."

The blue cattle truck stopped beside a huge herd of sheep. Bunabun, the ranch hand who worked for the owner of East Slope Three tending the many herds of sheep, looked at the sea of wooly animals around him.

He was told to load six of the rams on the truck and it didn't matter which ones they were, but he still dreaded it. Full grown male sheep get very touchy and easily irritated, and they get mean if they take a notion. And they usually take a notion.

The female sheep, the ewes, would be a lot easier to load, but he needed to load rams to make the story come out right. The story he and Jungili had made up must come out right in the event he was stopped.

Bunabun was nervous but there was really no reason for it. There was no reason why this plan would not work, just like it had in the past, even if he was questioned. He didn't like doing this, but just a few more successful trips and he would be a very rich man. He would do his part, and Jungili would do his, and they would both be rich.

Bunabun coaxed the rams toward the truck. A helicopter going overhead did not help matters but then it didn't hurt much, either. These rams had never wanted to go where they were supposed to go so this was no different, but he would need to just keep at it. He'd get them in there.

The worse thing, actually, was these stupid, bone-headed kangaroos bouncing around, disturbing the sheep. Helicopters were not as much of a bother as the kangaroos, but nothing could be done about either of them. It was impossible to fence out the kangaroos or the airplane. So it was best to ignore them.

Bunabun amused himself with his thoughts. He could laugh about all this trouble when he was rich and could leave these dumb, stinking sheep and this hot, dusty ranch. He would go to Adelaide where things were happening. Finally he got the rams loaded.

As he was driving toward the opal mine, the noisy, clap-clapping helicopter came over again. What was the reason for all this activity? Were the ranch owners suspicious about the truck being out in the field? Were the mine owners suspicious about the mine? Had the Englishman, Mr. Longley, seen something he shouldn't have seen? Well, either way, it was too late to do anything now, whatever the problem was.

He rehearsed his story. He, Bunabun, the hard working ranch hand, was merely transferring these six breeding rams over to East Slope Nine and he would be bringing six rams from that herd back to this herd. In this way, the bloodlines would be established that would bring better lambs to both flocks.

It was Jungili's idea of a story but it was better than any story he could have thought up. There! He now had the story straight in his mind, just in case he was stopped. But what if it was the ranch owner up there in that little whirling machine? He would know the story was a lie. What then? No time to think of that.

As the helicopter passed over his head without incident, Bunabun relaxed. Along the rutted trail of a road that passed by the opal mine, Bunabun stopped the truck and got out. He walked to the rear of the truck to pretend he was examining a tire. He even let out a little air from the tire, just in case he was challenged. Then he took his tire changing equipment from the truck and put it on the ground beside the tire.

He looked quickly in all directions before walking over to the scrap pile where the rock chips were discarded. If all went well, ten minutes from now this would all be over and he would be speeding on his way. None too soon, either, because darkness was settling in. He knelt by the scrap pile and began examining the rocks.

Sally and Darla climbed to their upstairs room, bringing one of the lanterns with them. It was going to be dark soon and they would need the light to admire their pretty stones.

"There," said Darla, as she spread the rocks in a row. "Now you can choose first if you want, then I'll choose, then you and then me, and we'll each have the same number of rocks. What are you going to do with yours?"

"I haven't really thought about it yet. I expected to get only one little piece, if we were lucky, and I would put it away as a souvenir of this trip. But now I have more and I'd like to have even more than this. Is that being greedy?"

"Probably."

Sally wondered, "Do you think Uncle Monty would take us back to the pile so we could look for more?"

Darla considered the question. "I don't know. He's really busy and he still has the trip down to Tasmania to photograph their devil."

"DEVIL?"

Darla giggled. "Yes, the Tasmanian devil. He looks like a furry dog and has a very bad temper like a bobcat or wolf. But he's a marsupial and this film is to show the variety of pocketed animals in Australia and how they fill the ecological spot that other animals do in other countries."

"I see. But I never thought we would be photographing the devil."

"I know. I never expected to actually see the devil. Anyway, about the rocks, we can watch and see how things go. Maybe there will be time."

"Darla, I have an idea."

"What?"

"If we could stay here while they go shooting the next part, we could walk over there and have a lot of time to look. You remember Mr. Longley said we could have all the rocks we wanted, so it wouldn't be stealing."

"That sounds like a good idea, all right, but I don't think Dad would go for it. He's so funny about being safe, you know, after that time I was kidnapped in Mexico. But maybe we can think of something else."

"But what is there here that could hurt us?"

"Probably nothing, but you know how Dad is."

"Yes, you're right. But Darla, there are two of us now. If I had been with you in Mexico, the kidnappers wouldn't have grabbed you."

"Maybe. We'll just have to see."

"Darla, look out the window. The night-lights came on over at the mine. Isn't it pretty with the darkness around? It looks a lot like when they drill a new oil well back home. Remember the lights strung up in the tower and the other lights moving around the drill rig at night?"

"But, look, Sally, they must be going to work at the mine tonight. Someone is coming in a truck. See the outline of it against the lights?"

"Truck? Why would they need a big truck for those tiny stones?"

"I don't know. Look, it isn't moving at all and it really isn't at the mine. Or is it?"

"I thought it was. No, see the light? There's a little light moving around like they're looking for something."

"I'll bet he had a flat tire, and he's looking for one of the little bolts or nuts he has to have to put the tire back on."

"Well, he's going to get help."

"How so?"

"Look over at the mine. Someone with a lantern is coming over to him."

"Good. I'd hate to have trouble all alone on one of those little old roads."

The girls turned away from the window. "I wish I could think of something really neat to do with these little rocks," Darla sighed.

"Maybe we just need to get our minds off them. Hey, I thought of something."

"What?"

"How do koalas sleep?"

"Let's look out the window and see if we can see them."

The girls leaned out the tiny upstairs window, blinking to look up into the dark branches.

"Look, there's a bump on the branches but I don't think we can get the lantern to shine up that high."

Darla agreed. "We need the spotlights Dad uses. I'll go get them. Maybe we could take pictures right now. DAD? We want to film the koalas now. Can we?" Darla called as she descended the ladder.

Soon everyone was upstairs crowding into the small room. A spotlight was attached to the side of the window and the beam of light was aimed toward the dark bump on the limb. The bump became a gray-furred animal sitting firmly in the fork of a branch. The koala turned its head to stare at the intruders but did not seem to be overly disturbed by the light.

"She's tame, Dad. Was she someone's pet, do you think?"

"Uncle Monty, may I hold the camera?"

"You surely may. Sally, do you see that large limb just below the window? I want you to step down there on that limb and I'll hand you the camera. That way we can get a different angle on her."

"I'm going out there, too."

"Wait, Darla." Her father cautioned. "We don't know how strong these limbs are and it's a long way to the ground."

The spotlights made clear pictures of the little animal against the blackness of the sky. Sally moved to another limb and Darla stepped out of the window to follow her. It was very dark now. With blackness above and blackness below, the spotlights made a small island of light among the limbs of the eucalyptus tree.

While the girls took pictures from several angles, the photographer watched from the window. "Sally, step up to that next limb. The koala does not seem to be upset by you girls so we might try to get a little closer. Now be careful where you step."

"I'm always careful, Uncle Monty. Here, Darla, hand me the camera. I can get a good shot from here."

Darla lifted the camera to Sally and glanced toward the opal mine. "Look, Dad, that sheep hauler is having trouble. He's been looking for something on the ground and it looks like he hasn't found it yet. We thought he might have had a flat but he's had more than enough time to fix it."

Mr. Wentworth agreed. "Looks like you're right. Perhaps I should go over there and see if I can help. You girls come back inside now. I believe we have enough of this angle. Danny, you come with me and we'll swing over there. Dennis, you stay here."

"Aw, Dad...."

"You heard me. I don't like to leave you alone, but three people are safer than two, most of the time," his father said as he came down the ladder.

The chopper blades began their clap-clap and the engine roared. The aircraft lifted off the runway with its ground lights flooding the runway, making the ground as light as though it was daytime.

The truck was only a short distance away, and the lights would make it a lot easier to spot the truck from the air. Bunabun stood beside the cattle truck, wearily rubbing his eyes. "Where are they?" he complained. "That's all I want to know. Just where are they? I should have been a long way down the road by now."

Jungili, who knelt of the ground, raked his hands through the scrap rock pile one more time. "But they were here, I tell you. I put them all together on this side of the pile, just like before."

"But they're not here, just like before. And I went to a lot of trouble to load the woolliest rams I could find. We could hide a house in the hair on the back of these beasts and now you can't even find some little old rocks."

"Just a minute. They have to be here," insisted the kneeling man.

Then suddenly he stood up to face the other man. "Bunabun, you are trying to double-cross me! I'll bet you have those opals already hidden and you're trying to tell me you don't have them. I'll bet you were going to sell them and keep all the money," accused Jungili, angrily.

Bunabun shrugged. "See for yourself if I'm lying, but I have to be getting on. I've been gone too long as it is."

Jungili climbed the wide rails and felt in the shoulder wool of the nearest ram. The shoulder was covered with thick, greasy wool, but that was all.

At that moment the clap-clap of the helicopter sounded overhead and the engine of the blue truck roared up into action.

"Jump out!" yelled Bunabun to the man in the truck. "I'm getting out of here. Something isn't right and I'm not going to stay around and see what it is." And with that, he jumped into the truck and gunned the motor. He jammed his foot into the accelerator and the truck shot down the dark road with Jungili hanging on the side rails.

The truck was already going too fast for Jungili to attempt to jump, so he climbed back over the rails and into the truck bed with the rams. At the speed Bunabun drove, and as rough as the road was, Jungili was forced to struggle to hold on and avoid being stepped on by the excited rams. The truck was speeding through the darkness, bouncing up and down and swaying from side to side. Bunabun had not turned on his headlights. Perhaps he could lose the helicopter if he drove in the dark and did not use his headlights. Then the aircraft would not have anything to guide it.

Overhead, Mr. Wentworth and Danny saw the truck pull away in the darkness.

"It was the lights, Dad." Danny decided. "They were trying to get the lights to work, but now he decided to go on in the dark."

"You may be right, Son. That's something we can certainly help him with. We'll just follow along overhead with the ground lights shining down and then he can see where's going."

The truck sped on down the road. When things started to go wrong, they just kept on getting worse, Bunabun decided. Where could he go? That helicopter seemed determined to follow. It had him pinned down with the spotlight.

Every turn he made caused the chopper to turn with him. Should he stop? Should he drive faster? No, the chopper could easily outdistance him. Should he drive on to East Slope Nine and hope for a good idea to happen in his head? Would he …what?"

"Look, Dad, the lights came on! We can go back now, can't we?"

They followed for a little space and the truck lights stayed on.

"Look! He must have had a short in the electrical system and a bump in the road made them come back on again. He should be all right now, shouldn't he?"

"Yes, unless another bump shuts them off again. However, I agree that we can go back now. Chances are he'll make it to wherever he's going."

With these words, he swung the helicopter around and headed back to East Slope Three.

In the back of the cattle truck, Jungili crouched down among the sheep. Bunabun seemed not to care how bumpy the road was or how sharply he turned the corners. The rams swayed against the side rails and scrambled with their sharp little hoofs to keep from falling down. They stepped on his feet and shoved him against the rails, fairly squeezing the breath out of him, but he couldn't stand up. The spotlight in the chopper would shine on him and he'd never be able to explain why he was riding in the back of a truck with a bunch of rams. Bunabun must be right about that chopper. It had to be a government agent sent out here to check on the theft of opals.

Jungili thought fast as he clung to the side rails of the truck. *As quick as the chopper stops,* he promised himself, *I will jump over the side and run, and get as far away from the truck as possible. It'll take a little while for the agent to get from the chopper to the truck and that will give men time to get away. They won't find any opals, and it won't help Bunabun for me to be caught. In fact, he might have trouble explaining me, so it'll be better if I run.* It seemed like a good plan.

With the plan now made, he concentrated on not being crushed by the stinking rams. Then, all in one clear flash of knowledge, he knew where the opals were. Why hadn't he figured it out sooner?

Those pesky children had rummaged through the scrap pile this afternoon, and they would have spotted the real opals in a minute. Everything was perfectly clear, now that it was too late. Any minute now, the loud speaker would come on in the chopper and the agent would command Bunabun to stop.

Then suddenly Bunabun turned on the truck lights. Whatever was he thinking of? By then, what did it matter? They had been spotted anyway, and now he had to think of getting away.

But no! Look at that chopper. It was circling to go back. It was probably going after back-up help. No, that wouldn't be right. If it was an agent after criminals, which they were, they would have all the help they needed right there in the chopper. So what was going on? He had to get Bunabun stopped now before he, Jungili, got any farther away from where he was supposed to be than he was already.

Jungili pushed his way forward through the woolly animals to the cab of the truck and pounded his fists against it.

Bunabun stopped and got out, yelling, "What are you doing back there? I told you to jump out back at the mine."

"But I didn't, and now I know where the opals are."

"Sure you do. We just spent an hour looking, remember?"

Jungili let that insult pass. "But I know now."

"So let's go get them and hush the chatter."

"We can't."

"Why not?"

"Those girls from East Slope Three cabin took them."

"Girls? How would they get them?"

"Oh, that chopper pilot brought four half-grown kids over to tour the mine. One of the girls took pictures and Longley told them they could have any of the scrap rocks they wanted."

"And they got the opals?"

"They must have. Where else would they be?"

"So, what now?"

"We'll just have to get them back. The people will leave the cabin empty to go flying around, and we'll just have to go search it."

"When will it be empty?"

"Now, how would I know that? Am I magic or something? If I was magic, I would make those stones be in my hand right now. No, we'll just have to wait and watch and catch them gone. Then we can go in and search."

"How long will that take? I've had this truck too long already."

"You'll have to take it back and get it again. Do I have to do all the thinking for you?"

"I don't know if I can do what you said," responded Bunabun stubbornly. "The boss man will be suspicious."

"Stop worrying about it. That's what you have to do. Right now you have to take me back to the mine so I can get some sleep and be there in the morning."

In the attic room at East Slope Three, Darla and Sally made their plans.

"If we go down to Tasmania on Thursday," outlined Darla, 'that gives us two days here. One day Dad wants to go film the bandicoot and we'll want to go with him. The other day will be for the kangaroos."

"I don't care so much about going on that trip," admitted Sally, "but I really would like to see those nine inch kangaroos."

"Me, too, but I don't think they're in this area. I really want to take some more pictures of the koala. I want to get a lot of pictures that are so good that Dad will use for film in the documentary. That means they would have to be very good."

"We could see if he'd let us stay here while he goes to film the kangaroo. Is that what you're thinking?" suggested Sally.

"That might work, but even if he did, he'd make us promise to stay inside the cabin and out of sight while he was gone."

"That's right, and then we couldn't walk over to the rock pile."

"I have it!"

"What?"

"If we do the koala pictures and do a really good job, then Dad would have more time. Then he would take us over there when he got back. That would work."

"Hey, yeah! But would he trust us to take good pictures? Remember, we haven't done this very much."

"I know, but if we took a lot of shots, he could review them and later cut away our mistakes. Dad says the shots are the only cheap part of photography. Lights, lens and location cost a lot more than anything else."

Sally nodded. "We could ask him, anyway."

"I've decided what to do if I get a lot of rocks."

"What?"

"If I had some of the bigger ones and some mortar or strong glue, I could put them together and make a tiny wishing well with a chain and little bucket. I could use it for pins and hair fasteners."

"That would be a good idea. I think I'd like to make a tiny rock house with a wooden roof. I'd make a little slot in the roof and use it for a bank."

A voice came up from downstairs. "Go to sleep, girls. Cut out the whispering."

"All right, Dad."

"Good night, Uncle Monty."

The next morning Mr. Wentworth's biscuits were even more delicious than usual. Stuffed full of sausage, they were delectable. Spread with butter and strawberry jam, they were scrumptious.

"Dad, toss me another biscuit, please."

The biscuit came sailing over the small table and Dennis fielded it expertly. "Can I toss him the jam, Dad?" Danny held a spoonful of the red mixture above his head.

"Put it down, Danny."

"All right, Dad. I was just trying to help."

"More sausage, please," requested Sally."

"Dad?"

"Yes, Kitten?"

"Sally and I want to take the shots of the koala."

"Certainly, Darla. You may help."

"But Dad, we want to do it all."

"We'll see."

Darla waited a minute. "Dad, we wanted to do it all. Alone."

"Why?"

Darla drew in a deep breath. "Well, Dad, we have two reasons, really. I want to be able to say we did it all alone, but we also wanted to save you some time. While you're doing the kangaroos, we can do the koala."

"I really believe we'll have time for everything, don't you?"

Darla shook her head.

"What do you want, Kitten? Just ask for it."

"More rocks."

"More rocks? But don't you have a lot?"

"Yes, but we each want a little sack full."

"We? Sally wants a sack full, too? Getting a little greedy, are we? Now I see why you two were trying to be helpful."

"Oh, no, Dad. We want to shoot the koala even if we don't get to stay here alone."

"Alone? Say, now, that's another problem…."

Dennis, with his mouth full, put in, "Leave them here, Dad."

Danny agreed. "They'll just be in the way if we take them along."

"Please, Dad?" We'll promise to stay inside the cabin and no one will ever know we're here. We can get a lot of good shots right out the window."

"Please?"

"Oh, don't say 'no'!"

The photographer looked from one to the other. He was clearly outvoted but safety was the big issue. Let's see. No one knew they were here except the people at the mine, and they would certainly be no threat. Then, of course, if the chopper was not setting beside the cabin, it would be assumed that everyone in the family was gone with it. Maybe. No, he shouldn't take such a chance here in a totally foreign country, But… they were all looking up at him with pleading eyes. Why not?

"I'll think about it," he told them.

"Oh, thank you, Daddy."

The photographer looked around the table at the four of them. Apparently he had already done his thinking and he had made the right decision because they were all happy with it.

"But girls, before we leave, I want to set up the time exposure, wide angle lens to snap every 10 seconds. We'll set it outside the cabin aimed up at the koalas and then we'll have a continuous story of the morning's activities in the tree and you may experiment with other shots."

Darla nodded happily. "Fine, Dad." She could tell that he didn't really trust them to do a good job, but that was understandable. This was actually Dad's job and it was his responsibility to make the films really good because the customer had to pay a lot of money for them. But they would show him, she and Sally, and they would get some first class, really good pictures.

Mr. Wentworth set the camera in a camouflaged position, though he wondered why he tried to disguise it. The koalas certainly didn't seem to mind anything they did, and paid no attention at all. They just sat in the tree forks and munched leaves.

Then he took a final look at the girls and decided he was just being overprotective. Actually, they would be fine alone.

All the necessary gear was loaded into the chopper and it lifted off in search of the most active band of kangaroos.

Darla and Sally watched the aircraft grow small in the distance, then, eyes twinkling, they grinned happily at each other. They were all alone to do the filming, and they would also get more of the colorful rocks! It was going to be a wonderful day!

They began the festivities by having one more biscuit with strawberry jam, and by drinking up the last of the reconstituted, powdered orange juice.

They had been so sure they would be permitted to stay that they had not bothered to get dressed. Darla was wearing her gray knit joggers and Sally was in her pink and blue striped pajamas.

"I want to climb all the way up to the mama koala and see if there are any babies in her pocket."

"But what if she scratches you? Her claws are very long, and she might even knock you out of the tree."

"I don't think so. I can climb faster than she can. Why, just look at her. She's slow as molasses in January."

"But you've never felt in her pocket. She might resent that, and she might knock you out of the tree. Then I'd have to go out to drag you back in and I promised Uncle Monty I wouldn't go outside."

"All right, I'll not upset her," promised Darla. "I'll just tell her I'm going to make a movie star out of her. Just think! She'll be in a film for thousands of people to see!"

"How do you know if it's a lady koala? It might be a fellow."

Darla chuckled. "I guess I'll know that when I find out if she has a pocket."

"But, either way, we're going to make her a star."

"Sure. I can hear her now, bragging to all her friends about being in a foreign movie."

"Foreign?"

"Sure. We're foreigners here, you know, so if she is in our film, it will be a foreign film to her."

"Let's do it now. Shall we put on our jeans?"

"No, that would take too long. No one is coming, I hope."

"Right. Let's go up and look at her and we can decide what to do first."

Bunabun hid the blue cattle truck in a dry ditch under some tall trees. He was no doubt already in trouble because he had kept the truck so long, so he might just as well keep it and do what had to be done. They probably would question why he needed it so soon after bringing it in, and might not let him have it. He couldn't risk that happening.

He piled a few limbs over the bright blue cab of the truck. The government agent, or whoever it was, could fly by at any time and it was never good to be seen in a place where he had no reason to be. He'd have to think up a good story for being so late.

Bunabun sighed as he put another limb on the truck. Sometimes he felt the ranch foreman was spying on him and he'd have to be more careful or he would get himself fired. However, the risk was worth it because just a few more trips like this one and he wouldn't need their old job! Then he would have a lot of money and just watch out then! 'Adelaide, here I come!' and there would be fun the rest of his life!

Anyway, the truck was now well hidden. It made him tired and thirsty, and for whatever it mattered, he hated sheep, too. He wasn't supposed to have to do all this. That was not the agreement. All he had to do was drive those sheep by the mine, pickup up those little rocks the foreigners liked so well and hide them in the thick wool of the sheep. Then he would drive them to East Slope Nine and they would be someone else's problem. He'd get his money, then.

Simple. Only that was not the way this trip had worked out and it was all because of the pesky kids and the fellow in the chopper.

Not only had the rocks not been where they were supposed to be, now he had to go help Jungili find them and he hadn't been the one who lost them. It was not fair. He hoped he could get this business over and done with quickly.

Jungili, instead of standing guard in the mine as he was paid to be, had slipped away under the cover of bushes and through dry ditches. He hurried, knowing Bunabun was already waiting to go with him to search the cabin by the airstrip. It was a shame this problem had come up, just when everything was going good. Of course, it was not because of anything he had done. He had put the stones where he always did, but they just didn't stay there. Now it was up to him to get the plan working again. The whole idea was not good, but there was no time to make up a better one, so he'd just have to stick with it.

Yes, he told himself, it was really going good, considering that this was the fourth time he had removed a number of expensive stones. He transported them to East Slope Nine, where an accomplice shipped them out, wrapped in small packages on the mail plane. No one suspected him of anything. The stupid Mr. Longley couldn't see what was going on right before his nose.

Now that this problem had happened, he probably should make a new plan. But then, after a lot of thought, he had decided the helicopter pilot was not the law coming to get them, and that the silly children really did not know the value of the rocks they had most certainly picked up from the scrap pile.

For a while there, he had been concerned that the girl had photographed the cart, but she would not get the pictures printed until much later, and by that time everything would be over. But why were they here? Vacationers, no doubt. Foreigners took vacations. Well, when he had a lot of money, he would move to Adelaide, and that would be better than a vacation for him. No more work in the mine and no more Mr. Longley looking over his shoulder.

It was good that Bunabun was already near the cabin. They had no time to lose because the chopper with the man and the children was gone and would be back, who knows when, and they must have their search completed and be gone by then. No reason to complicate matters by being caught snooping where he had no business to be.

"Come on, Bunabun," he called. "Let's hurry."

"Listen to him," Bunabun told the kookaburras, flapping their silly wings and screeching overhead. "He says 'hurry' and I've been waiting for him for hours! Let's go."

Together the men hurried across the flat Australian pasture land. As small as the cabin was, it wouldn't take long to search. The stones were sure to be laying some place easy to see.

Darla and Sally had scrambled up the ladder to the attic. The sun was in a very good position for filming. It shone brightly down through the leaves, dappling and flickering its light below the limbs. Now where was that koala?

Sally leaned out the window to take a look. "Oh, Darla! There's another one out here."

"Another what?"

"Koala. Look, it has a bump hanging on its neck. Oh, it's a baby! And that's what we wanted! We can get a really good close up of the baby. I'm climbing out."

"Wait, I'll go, too."

"You hold the camera while I step out on the limb. See, Darla, there's another koala up there."

"Wait, Sally," commanded Darla.

"I'll be all right. Here, hand me the camera."

"Come back. Sally. Hurry! Right now!"

Sally stepped back through the window. "What's wrong with you? It was all right for us to climb out there last night. Remember, Uncle Monty let us?"

"It's not that. Look, Sally."

"Where?"

"Through the trees there. Men. See them?"

"Oh, my! I wonder if they saw me. Or heard me!"

"Yeah, and I wonder where they're going. There isn't any place to be walking to around here. There's only the mine and they don't seem to be going in that direction."

"I wish Uncle Monty was here. My heart is pounding."

"Wait, Sally. Doesn't one of those men look like that foreman back at the mine?' Mr. Jingle, or something like that, Mr. Longley called him?"

"I don't remember, Darla. Look, they're coming here."

"Looking for Dad?"

"I don't think so. They wouldn't think he was here because the chopper isn't here. But we're here."

"What then?"

"Maybe they want him to be gone?"

"Hide! We've got to."

"Where?"

"Under the beds."

"No, they'd see us there. Lumpy, remember?"

"Then where? Hurry and think. They're just outside."

"We've got to do something," insisted Darla. "We can't let them know we're in here."

"Jump out the window?"

"And break a leg? And start crying? Then they'd find us for sure."

"Climb on the roof?"

"That's a good idea. You're still in pajamas. Hurry and get into your gray jogging suit. That pink and blue shows up too well."

Sally stripped off her pajamas and tossed them on the bed. She stepped into her gray jogging shorts and pulled the top over her head.

Darla stood by the window. "They're in the yard now," she whispered. "We'll have to wait until they get around the corner of the house so they won't see us climb out."

Darla stood by the window with one foot on the windowsill, ready to step out on a limb. Sally was close behind her. They heard the knock-knock as the men rapped on the cabin door. They heard other noises and someone talking in a low voice, too low to understand.

Finally, Darla stepped carefully out onto the limb and began to climb upward. Sally stepped quietly out behind her.

Then they heard the cabin door open and then bang shut. They heard footsteps and other noises as the men shuffled around through the baggage and supplies.

"Hurry and get over on the roof," Sally encouraged in a whisper.

"I'm afraid to," Darla whispered.

"Then I'll go first."

"It isn't that."

"Then what?"

"The grass roof is slick and there isn't anything to hold on to. When I try to get a hold of it, the grass just breaks off in my hand." Darla dropped a handful of grass to prove it.

"Oh, don't do that," warned Sally. "They might see the grass fall past the window."

"What can we do?"

"Can you just step over to the roof and kind of work your foot into it? You could hold to that limb over there."

Darla grasped the overhead limb and pushed her foot into the grass. It crackled terribly loud. She pushed a little harder and her foot poked all the way thorough into the attic room.

"We can't do it, Sally. We'll have to stay in the tree."

"Oh, my! What if they see us and shoot us?"

"I guess it won't be any worse than standing on the ground and being shot. Come on, let's climb."

Darla climbed up limb after limb, hugging the trunk of the tall tree. Sally chose a large limb and crawled out, wrapping her legs around the rough bark.

The girls could hear the voices of the men inside the house, but not well enough to understand what they said. There was a lot of slamming of suitcases and equipment. They both cringed at the noise, wondering what was being broken.

Then the voices became clearer as the men climbed the ladder.

"They'd be up here. I see girl stuff laying all around," came the voice from inside.

Sally's eyes got wide as she looked up at Darla. The men were indeed looking for them. They had to be, because she and Darla were the only 'girls' around. Why had she chosen to crawl out on a limb rather than climbing high, like Darla? But it was too late now. She squeezed herself into as small a person as she could, pulling her legs up under her. She kept forgetting to breathe and then she got dizzy. She couldn't afford to get dizzy because then she would fall. *Breathe*, she told herself.

Still as a stone on a mountaintop she stayed. Then she saw that she was not alone on the limb. Creeping up behind her was the furry mama koala with the baby clinging to her neck. The animal crawled slowly along the limb, getting closer and closer to Sally.

Words came from the window. "Here's hair things and toothbrushes and girls' clothes but there are not any rocks," complained one voice.

"But they have to be here. The girls liked those rocks," put in another voice.

"They must have liked them, because they took them quick enough."

"They're just not here."

"They have to be."

"But you can see, they're not."

"Look again. We have to have those rocks."

Darla looked down at Sally. Sally's eyes were bright with understanding. Rocks? Valuable? Somehow their scrap 'rocks' had become real opals. How could that be?"

Darla had turned pale with fright and Sally was now as gray as her jogging suit.

The koala mother moved slowly up the limb. Her gray furry head nudged gently against Sally's gray clad backside. In koala language, the nudge probably meant, "Excuse me, please, and move over because I want to pass you."

Sally would have been glad to move over but there was no place to move to, and she was scared stiff. The mama nudged her again. This was getting serious.

Sally turned her head to look at the furry animals and when she did, her hands lost their grip on the limb. She instantly curled her leg over the limb and gripped it tightly with her knees. It was very uncomfortable. The rough bark dug into her flesh through the thin knit of the clothes, but she hung there under the limb, looking like a three-toed sloth, just having his breakfast.

The mama koala watched her, and apparently Sally had done what was expected of her, because here she came with the baby, moving slowly up the limb and over Sally's legs. The sharp claws of the mama dug into Sally's knees as she climbed on out to the end of the limb.

One claw clasped Sally's arm where she held to the limb. Sally tried to hold still but the pain made her flinch. The mama koala slipped a little, and stepped one foot down into Sally's face to steady herself. Then she went on, but the baby loosened its grip on it's mother's fur and dropped gently to Sally's stomach. Mother crawled on while the baby clung to Sally's gray knit suit.

The whole thing wouldn't have been so bad because the baby was not heavy at all, but its little sharp claws pierced the fabric of Sally's clothes and it was clinging tightly to the skin of Sally's stomach. It partly hurt and partly tickled, but something had to be done about it right now! Immediately!

With a quick jerk, Sally drew herself back up on to the limb. Let the baby fall where it would. She couldn't help that.

But the baby did not fall. It still held to Sally's shirt with its tiny, sharp claws, then began to climb slowly up to her neck. Then over into her hair. If the baby's claws had been sharp on her stomach, they were now like needles in her hair!

Sally eased up to a sitting position and quietly removed the baby with one hand, hooking him to a limb, just as one would hang an ornament on a Christmas tree limb. He actually seemed pleased to have something solid to hang onto after Sally's squirming body and loose clothing. He continued to look at Sally with his shiny bead eyes, as she clung to the limb like a gray bump.

Sally sighed gently with relief, and leaned down once more to make herself as little as possible.

There were voices again.

"It's no use. We've looked in every corner. There are no rocks here."

"But they've got to be here."

"But they're not."

So far, so good for the girls in the tree. They had managed to be silent and still, but at that very moment, the eucalyptus tree was visited by a pair of birds. Two Australian kookaburras fluttered clumsily thorough the leaves to a large limb, scuffling and squawking noisily and dropping a snowstorm of feathers.

Sally cringed at the noise and squeezed up into an even smaller ball of gray.

One of the voices demanded, "What is that noise?"

The other voice said, "Just a stinking bird in that tree."

The first voice demanded again, "So look out the window. The people might be coming."

The other voice advised, "I don't hear the chopper."

"Go look, anyway," came the command. "We can't let them catch us here or they will have the law on us."

"Oh, all right."

Heavy footsteps came noisily across the floor. The girls did not move. Neither did they dare to breathe.

"What's out there?"

With his head still out the window, the man answered. "There's nothing out here but stinking birds and a tree full of crawling koalas."

"Then get back in here and help me hunt."

The head disappeared inside the window.

"They're not here, I tell you, and I don't have time to be looking any longer. I'm going to be missed over at the mine and you've got to get this truck back if we ever expect to use it again."

"I sure hate to give up."

"But we have to."

The voices became faint as the men descended the ladder. Then a few loud words and they left the house, slamming the door behind them.

The men walked through the eucalyptus grove and directly under the tree where the girls clung. The girls could see them clearly. One of the men was certainly Mr. Longley's foreman, the one named Mr. Jingle, or something like that.

When the men were tiny figures in the distance, the girls uncurled their legs from the limbs and climbed back toward the attic window.

"Do you think they might come back?" Sally suggested.

"I don't think so. All they wanted was our rocks and they didn't find them. They certainly looked for them long enough," Darla decided.

"Isn't it lucky we put them in the box with the granola bars?' Sally giggled softly. "If they'd only been hungry, they'd have found them."

Darla chuckled. "Maybe they didn't think the granola bars were food. Not everyone is like Dad, who thinks it would be impossible to live well without granola bars to snack on."

Sally dug her hand into the box. "They're here, all safe and sound."

"But, Sally, these are real opals. We have real, valuable opals."

"Yeah, isn't it neat? And they really were given to us!"

"But Mr. Longley was tricked. He didn't intend to give them to us. They weren't supposed to be where they were."

"But that's not our fault. Then, of course, it wasn't his fault, either. I know that."

"So they really aren't ours."

"But nobody knows."

"That still doesn't make them ours."

"You're right. And there are three of us who know."

"Yeah: you, me and God."

Darla agreed. "Of course, I knew we couldn't keep them. I just wanted to think about it for a little while."

"Me, too, but we can still get some of the others," reminded Darla. "We can still do what we wanted to do with colored rocks. After all, that's what we thought we had, so what's the difference?"

"You're right. Oh, Sally, guess what?"

"We haven't taken the pictures. Where's the camera?"

"Right here behind the box where I hid it. I'm glad they didn't take it."

The girls raced back up the ladder. "Here, Sally, let me have the camera. You crawl out there and I'll hand it to you. We can get some really good pictures of that baby."

Sally sighed. "I just hope it can remember who its mama is. Not me, anymore!"

"Why, Sally, I thought you made a good mama!"

The baby koala had found his mama and was clinging firmly to her neck fur when they reached him. The camera recorded his bland expressions and his movement. It recorded the care the mother took as she selected one leaf for eating and turned another one down. Each leaf was examined before it was put in her mouth. Sometimes the mama did not want even the tiny, new leaves. The ones she did want, she turned over and over with her awkward claws before delicately munching them.

After a while, the baby either got hungry or tired because he worked his way around his mother's chubby body and crawled into her pocket, head first.

The mother koala seemed to take no notice of him but continued to select leaf after leaf and examine it with her round, twinkly eyes.

"I think I'd get tired of eating the same thing every meal. How can they live on nothing but leaves? How do they get enough vitamins and minerals?"

"Maybe they don't."

"But they stay alive."

"Yeah, they're alive but they're really dumb. Cute as can be, but dumb."

"So you think vitamins could make them smarter?"

"Couldn't hurt."

"I guess we'll never know, will we?"

A tiny speck appeared on the western horizon. The speck got bigger and noisier and finally turned into a helicopter.

"Here they come! We got finished just in time."

The chopper landed on the airstrip and the photographer and the boys gathered the cameras and other equipment and came in the cabin.

"How did you girls get along?" he greeted them.

"Fine, Dad. We got good pictures. A mama koala and her baby came over to our tree because she wanted the baby's picture taken."

"Yeah, right!" Dennis challenged.

"You'll see!" his sister retorted, smugly.

"Very good. Girls, we can go over to the mine now and get your rocks. Go get in the chopper."

Darla looked at Sally. Sally nodded. "I've got them."

"Dad," Darla began, "These rocks are really opals. I'm not sure what happened but we got them by mistake and we have to take them back. And, Dad, Mr. Longley's foreman came over here and searched our cabin for them but he didn't find them."

"SEARCHED OUR CABIN?" yelled her father. "WHERE WERE YOU?"

"Don't worry, Uncle Monty. We climbed up in the tree and they didn't even see us."

"Oh, my!" groaned the photographer. "I knew I shouldn't have left you two alone."

"But nothing happened, Uncle Monty."

"We're just fine, Dad. Really."

It was hard to convince Mr. Wentworth that they were really all right, and it was just about as hard to give up the beautiful little stones. It was also hard to see Mr. Longley's disappointment when he heard about his foreman's involvement.

"I'll be watching him, now, and we'll get the proof that we'll need to convict him. This is a job for the law, and when I get the proof, I'll turn it over to them. Now you girls take your time and find the prettiest rocks you can."

They did, and if they weren't quite as pretty as the opals, at least they got a lot of them. They had brought an extra pair of socks with them to the mine to use as bags. Now the knit of the socks was lumpy and bulgy with stones.

For dinner, the girls made salmon patties from canned fish, crackers and powdered eggs. They browned them in sausage fat. They stewed tomatoes with onions and macaroni. It was a really big meal, but the excitement had made them extra hungry.

The Bible verses at devotion that night were special ones.

"I'm first," insisted Sally. "Mine is 'He will give His angels charge over thee to keep thee in all thy ways.' I'm glad we had angels today."

Dennis added, "Yeah, and being up in the tree like you were, the angels didn't have so far to come down, huh?"

"Actually, it was the kookaburras that came first," Darla put in. "They were very noisy and the men looked at them instead of looking up. Do you suppose the angels sent the birds? My verse is, 'God made every tree to grow, and the tree of life also.' For Sally and me, the eucalyptus was a tree of life, today."

"Very good. Who's next?"

Danny spoke up. Mine is 'Thou shalt not kill.' I know that verse was meant for humans, but I wish animals didn't have to die. Like the poisoned wombat."

"Good. Dennis?"

"'Thou shalt not steal.' That means opals and everything. I guess people will go on trying it, won't they?"

"I suspect they will, Dennis. My verse is, 'He that cometh unto me shall never hunger, and he that believeth on me shall never thirst'. In that verse, God promises to be everything we need, just at the time we need it. Now, off to bed and go to sleep quickly. We photograph bandicoots tomorrow."

The next day the girls helped with the filming, but it was rather dull compared to the excitement of the day before.

Even the trip to the island of Tasmania to photograph the snarling, wolf-like animal called the Tasmanian devil was tame after the koala day. Sometimes humans can be more frightening than animals.

The boys followed trails and crept through the trees with the cameras, but the girls stayed in the helicopter most of the time.

It was fun, though, when they photographed the little yellow-eyed, cat-sized cuscus. The tiny animals climbed through the trees eating fruit, leaves and even birds and lizards when it could catch them. The varied diet surely contained more vitamins and minerals and other food values than just a diet of leaves, and sure enough, the cuscus looked and acted a lot smarter than the koala, but it's hard to tell smartness just by looking. And acting.

The little cuscus was not a native of southern Australia, preferring the warmer climate of the north, but the animal preserve at Adelaide kept them there for their interest value, making sure they were protected from the cold.

That made it very handy for the photographers. Their color ranged from black to almost white, but the prettiest of all were the yellow ones with dark yellow patches, and they all had darling yellow noses and yellow rings around their eyes.

The wary little animals were not tame like the koalas and the boys were forced to climb and crawl through the trees to get good shots of them as they played and ate.

Back in Adelaide, the gear was packed aboard the jet that had brought them there. The pilot picked up the mic and asked, "Beechking ICU 2 to Adelaide Tower. Awaiting instructions for take off."

The answer came crackling through the radio, "Tower to Beechking ICU 2. Proceed north on runway two. Have a good flight and come back to Australia again soon."

The jet nosed its way into the Australian sky. White clouds floated beside them and under them. The pilot listened to music on his radio and the boys started a game of checkers, but went to sleep before either of them could win.

Darla and Sally counted their colored rocks again, dividing them equally just before they, too, went to sleep.

They did not hear their pilot ask Mexico City for landing instructions and they were reluctant to leave the Beechking when they were awakened. They were influenced, however, by their hunger and the availability of Mexican food. Real Mexican food prepared in Mexico.

Then they were in the air again. The boys managed a quiet game of checkers before going back to sleep, but the girls didn't even try to stay awake.

Finally the pilot turned off his music and picked up the mic. "Beechking ICU 2 to Springfield Tower. Come in Springfield."

A pleasant voice with a soft Missouri accent answered, "Springfield Tower to Beechking ICU 2. Go ahead."

Then they were on the ground. They transferred their gear to the van they had left parked at the airport. Forty five minutes later they were at home again in Branson, Missouri. As much fun as these trips were, it was still nice to get home again.

The photographer had what was certainly millions of pictures that might even stretch across the whole state of Missouri if they were printed out! These would make a perfect pictorial comparison study of the interesting pocketed animals.

One evening not long after that, four pairs of eyes watched the photographer show his film for the first time.

The first shot was of the kangaroos grazing with the sheep on the Australian plains. Some of them bounced on their bony back legs, balancing themselves with their long, thick tails. They looked like tan grains of popcorn among the dull colored sheep.

Then the scene changed to a herd of grazing bison. The scenes of the American 'buffalo' had been taken some time ago on an American ranch. Then came herds of cattle grazing on the same ranch.

These were the native grass eaters, the kangaroos in Australia and the bison in America. Next came the South American llama and the African hippo. These animals all ate grass, but only the kangaroo kept her baby in her pocket.

Then, on the screen, came the rat-like bandicoot with its whiskers, pointed nose and long, almost hairless tail. There was absolutely nothing about this animal that could be said to be pretty. Its name in the Australian language means 'pig-rat' because of its appearance, but actually it is neither. The bandicoot is an insect eater as well as a nibbler of vegetation to supplement its diet. Neither pigs nor rats are primarily insect eaters.

After the bandicoot came the pictures of the American raccoon which had been taken while the family had camped on the rocky mountain range, filming a watershed. The raccoon peered at the camera with his shiny, beady eyes. He lifted his lip in a snarl, showing needle sharp teeth.

The next picture showed a mother raccoon with two babies. They were playing in a stream of water, catching crawfish. The mama raccoon would thrust her paw under a rock or log and a crawfish would grab onto it with its scissor claws. The mama raccoon would pull out her hand and eat the crustaceans off her fingers. One of the young ones did the same thing and was rewarded by a small shell fish that caught one of his 'fingers' but the other small one had no luck. He tried here and there, then turned to his mother in hunger and despair.

At that moment a very large set of claws caught his tail in a vice-like grip. The young raccoon whirled around, grabbed the crawfish with his 'hands,' then crunched greedily on the shellfish not bothering to remove it from pinching his tail.

The bandicoot, ugly as it was, occupied the same position in the food chain as the American raccoon and other small American animals. They all eat a little vegetation, but concentrate on insects, and only the bandicoot has the baby pocket. The one exception was the American opossum.

And there he was. Or rather, there she was. Ugly and gray with a pointed whiskery nose and hairless tail came the mother opossum. She was walking up a leaning log that had been a tree, storm-blown against another tree years ago. The opossum had babies on her back, clinging to her thick tail by their own tiny tails. Ugly and naked of hair, they were so terrible-looking that they were almost cute. They had pink skin and bright eyes.

Mama opossum walked up the rotting log, sniffing here and there. Then, at a certain decayed spot, she raked at the wood with her claws and the rotten wood fell away. There, inside the log, white specks were crawling about. The hungry mother animal licked up the termites, wiggling her lips to make sure all of the insects got inside her mouth. She looked, for all the world, like she should have come from Australia but they had taken her picture not a mile from their home in Missouri.

After the opossum came the wombat, stupid-looking with its nearsighted eyes. The photographer did not include the scenes showing the poisoned animal. Those pathetic shots would be saved for another film. These pictures were really good.

There were scenes inside the burrow, showing the face of the wombat in the dim light. There were other scenes of the animals coming out in the late evening for a night of foraging among the plants, and there were pictures of the mama nuzzling her baby away from the camera into the safety of her backward pocket. They were poor, slow-moving old wombats, but they had managed to survive for thousands of years.

Then came the American counterparts, the animals that filled the same ecological roles as the wombat.

First came the quick, chattering prairie 'dog' which is not a dog at all, even though it does a good imitation of a barking dog when it gets upset. The prairie dog makes burrows and eats grass roots, but it has so many enemies that it cannot afford to be slow like the wombat. Only the fastest of them stay alive and away from wolves and coyotes.

There was another interesting similarity between the wombat and the prairie dog. The wombat burrows in Australia were also inhabited by rabbits, who did not dig burrows themselves, but wanted a place to hide. The American prairie dog also had house guests. The western burrowing owl, which does not burrow, will, however, nest in the prairie dog runs.

But the prairie dog does not have a pocket for the baby. The babies are left in the nest until they are big enough to care for themselves. If the prairie dogs had to carry their babies around with them, they could not move fast enough to stay alive.

Also similar to the wombat was a woodchuck, sometimes called a marmot. The woodchuck was a slower-moving animal, more like its Australian counterpart. It also had the hairy coat and semi-hairy tail.

Then came the darling, furry cuscus, walking about in the tree, eating whatever it could find. Small insects were popped into its sharp-toothed mouth. Even a blue lizard was crunched, enjoyably.

("It looks like she's eating a stick of beef jerky," observed Dennis.)

The yellow-eyed cuscus selected twigs and leaves for nibbling, and, on one occasion, snipped off a flower bud and munched it.

After the cuscus, came the American marten, a sleek, long bodied animal with beautiful thick fur and a long tail, just like the cuscus. The marten walked about on the tree limbs, eating whatever it could find, even munching a bird egg or two.

The cuscus of Australia and the marten of America could almost appear to be cousins when comparing their diet and gracefulness, their tree-top hunting ground, and their agility, but there was one big difference. That difference was the baby pocket. It was the presence of the pocket that classified the cuscus as a marsupial.

Then came the koala. Darla and Sally had been waiting eagerly for the first sight of the scenes they had taken.

First came the scene against the dark sky that they had taken on the first night in the cabin. The little gray animal had turned to look down at Sally as she took the pictures.

There were scenes of the baby clinging to the mother's fur. Its eyes twinkled in the bright morning sunshine. The furry coats of the mother and baby shone silver and gray in the green of the eucalyptus tree.

Next came a shot of a slow-moving figure crawling up the main trunk of the tree. It was gray, but it was very long-legged. It kept looking nervously down toward the ground as another gray figure appeared in the tree.

The second figure crawled carefully out toward the end of a large limb.

"UNCLE MONTY, LOOK WHAT YOU DID! YOU PUT IN THE WRONG PICTURES!"

"DADDY, DON'T YOU DARE SHOW EVERYONE THOSE PICTURES OF US!"

But the scene continued. Just behind the gray figure came a mama koala with a baby clutching the fur of her neck. The mama butted her head gently against the gray figure on the limb, which wore no shoes on its bare feet.

Then the gray figure slipped, and everyone who watched it, caught a breath, but the gray figure held on. There it was, upside down, swinging like a sloth from the limb.

The mama koala crawled clumsily over the gray creature's feet and hands, and began to munch leaves.

The baby koala looked down at the swinging body of the larger gray animal and let loose of its mother's fur to drop down onto the other creature.

When the claws of the baby hit the creature's stomach, the creature made a terrible face, frowning and cringing. Carefully the large creature pulled itself up onto the limb with the baby gripping tightly. The larger creature let go of the limb and with its front 'paw' and seized the baby koala. The 'paw' pushed the baby against a tree limb and the baby's tiny claws hooked instantly to the bark of the tree.

Then the creature did a strange thing. It pulled its feet under it and wrapped its arms around the limb. Instantly, instead of being a clumsy land animal, it became a gray-furred koala hugging its tree-limbed home. Form the position of the camera, even looking closely, it would be hard to tell which was the real koala in the tree.

High in the tree, another of the larger 'koalas' hugged a limb and looked down.

"Look, Daddy, that's why the man didn't see us in the tree. We look just like big koalas. But, Dad…?"

"Yes, Kitten?"

"You can't leave those pictures in the documentary. This film is not supposed to be funny. And it's not about us."

The photographer grinned. "You just think I can't find an American equivalent to those strange Australian animals, don't you? Well, I believe I can find their equivalent right here in Missouri."

"Yeah, Dad, and look," Dennis put in. "They even have pockets. See there on the jogging suit? Man, what kooky koalas!"

"Dad, you wouldn't leave those in there, would you?"

"Well, Kitten, if you don't like that one, we can take it out and put this one in."

Now the screen showed pictures of the African monkeys climbing all around in tall trees, selecting this leaf and that tender stem to eat. Then came the monkeys of the South American rain forest by the Amazon River. The monkeys played and swung from limb to limb, but when they were hungry, they searched for young tender leaves just like their Australian counterparts.

Australia's pocketed animals found ways to use nature's resources just like animals from other continents.

The film had one last scene.

A pair of noisy kookaburras flew into a eucalyptus tree, scuffling and scrapping together in a shower of feathers. A dark-skinned face appeared and looked at the birds, then disappeared, never even noticing the large 'koalas.'

"Uncle Monty?"

"Yes, Sally?"

"Can I say my evening devotion verse now?"

"Let's hear it," invited her uncle.

"I would say, 'Thou preparest a table before me in the presence of mine enemies' only I would say it meant "Thou preparest a koala out of me in the presence of mine enemy,' because that is exactly what happened. Did you notice that?"

"Hey, yeah!" agreed Darla. "Isn't it lucky we were in jogging suits that were koala-colored? Then, it really didn't have to be luck. It could have been God and He doesn't need luck to make things come out right."

"Dad?"

"What, Dennis?"

"Let's leave those pictures in the film. We can tell people we discovered a new animal thought to be extinct."

Darla picked up a fizzy house slipper and flung it across the room, narrowly missing her brother. "One more remark like that and you may become permanently extinct."

"That's enough, kids."

Then Danny asked, "Dad, what are we going to do with the scenes of the sick wombat?"

"Well, Danny, that is a good question. We can put it with some scenes from other continents to show how 'un-human' we humans can be to our animals. It will be a sad documentary, but the truth is often sad, and we have to show it anyway.

"But there's one thing we are going to do with this film. We will send a copy to Mr. Longley, along with the one of the foreman and his buddy leaving the cabin. Then he'll have them to do whatever he needs to do."

"Are we through with this picture?"

"What picture will be next?"

"Do we have another assignment?"

"Actually, we have two assignments. We can go to the Arctic to count nesting sites of endangered sea birds."

"May we wait till the snow melts?"

"How long will it take?"

"Ten billion years."

"I'll wait. I don't like being cold."

"Then we have another assignment shooting life on the Ganges River in India."

"I vote for India," volunteered Sally.

"Kooky Koalas don't get a vote," Dennis teased.

The fuzzy house slipper flew across the room and this time it hit him squarely on the left ear!

- BONUS EXCERPT -

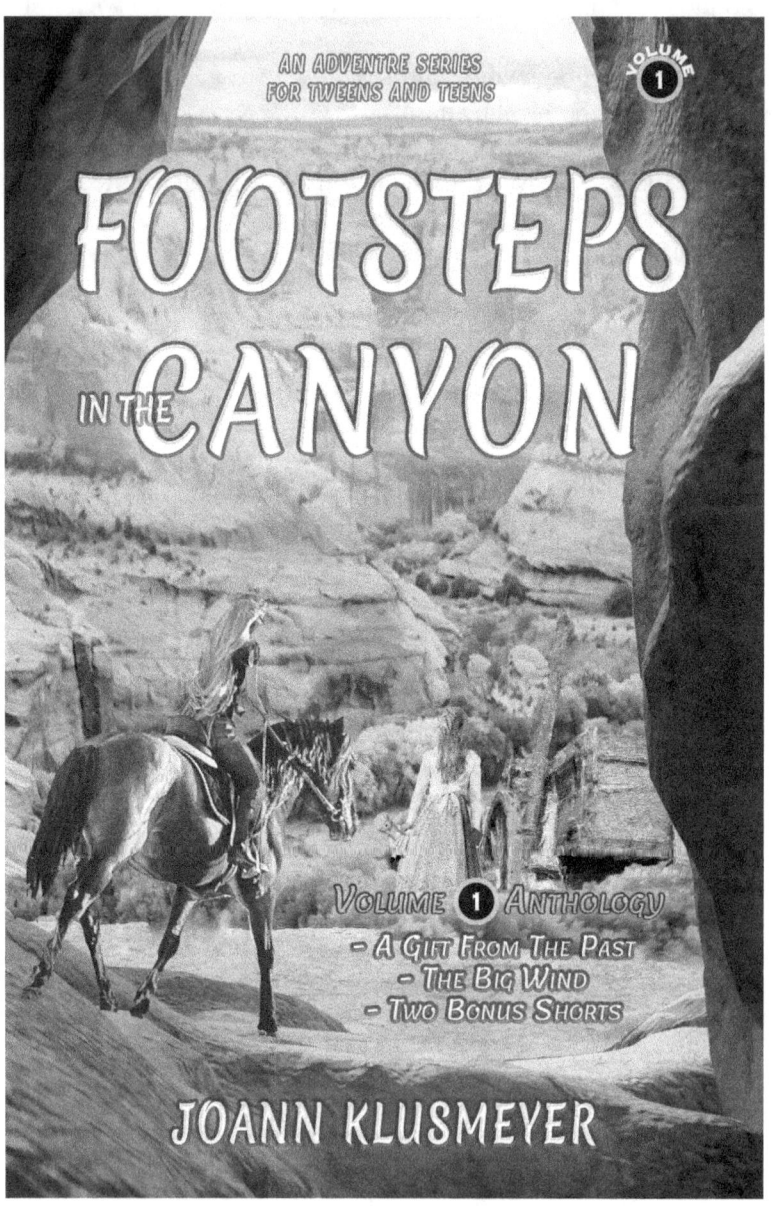

AN ADVENTRE SERIES
FOR TWEENS AND TEENS

VOLUME 1

FOOTSTEPS
IN THE CANYON

VOLUME 1 ANTHOLOGY
- A GIFT FROM THE PAST
- THE BIG WIND
- TWO BONUS SHORTS

JOANN KLUSMEYER

A GIFT FROM
THE PAST

High on the mesa sat the large ranch house, square and solid against the blue of the sky. Beside it were the three guest cottages and the long bunkhouse. Farther away were the buildings for the many kinds of animals. Fenced corrals surrounded the large barn, and many horses grazed in the pastures or stood dozing in the sun.

Thirteen-year-old Caitlyn Bradford yawned and rubbed her eyes. The bright sunshine outside her window called to her every time she looked away from the unfriendly face of the computer monitor. She had no way of knowing that this was a day that she would remember forever.

The lesson she had just downloaded, Beginning Algebra, was somewhat confusing, so she had put on the CD of the teacher's instructions, and now the lesson was no clearer than before. She decided the teacher didn't know how to do it either, so she must have studied long enough.

Home schooling from the Internet had its plusses, and it also had minuses. It meant you could study when you wanted to, and you could take a break when you got tired. It even meant that you could make the teacher "repeat" the instructions twenty times if you had trouble understanding something.

That's what home schooling had, but what it didn't have was other students. Caitlyn was always alone. Her bedroom was her classroom. The closest she got to other students was through email, except on picnic or party days, and they only came several times a year.

Clearly, it was time to treat herself with a break so she stepped outside. The sun seemed unusually bright after the dimness of the computer screen, but it instantly cheered her.

The "BB" name of the ranch was for her great grandfather Bradford and his brother, the original Bradford Brothers, but the neighbors had other names.

Other times it was the "BumbleBee", the "Bouncing Betty", and "Bouncing Bee" and even worse names sometimes. The official name was The Bradford Guest Ranch, but nobody cared.

Caitlyn hurried past the bunkhouse and went on to the stable where her horse might be. Then again, the horse might be in the corral, or in the near pasture. Josh Hunt would know. He always knew where every horse was at every minute. He knew because it was his job to know.

Josh was the head wrangler of the BB Ranch and he was in charge of the string of trail horses that were ridden by the ranch guests, and he also cared for all of the work horses. Probably forty animals in all, maybe more... and it was his job to keep up with them.

A loud whinny beside her ear told her where her palomino pony might be. The animal poked her golden head out of the half-door of the stable and whinnied again. She was ready for their afternoon ride.

"Hello, Golden," Caitlyn greeted the pony. "Are you ready?"

What a question! Of course she was ready. She had been ready and waiting for hours, so she tossed her head and snorted her answer!

Caitlyn tossed the light saddle over the back of the palomino. She had saddled her horse so many times that she could have done it in her sleep. It had been one of her father's rules. If she was big enough to ride, she was big enough to saddle and care for her horse without help from the wrangler. Even her little sister, Nelda, only ten years old, could saddle her own horse.

The girls had been told that Josh, the wrangler, had a job to do and he was not their servant, so the girls must care for their own horses. They brushed the animals and cleaned the stalls. That was the small price to pay for having their own horse to ride whenever they wanted to.

It seemed to be a good afternoon for a long ride, so Caitlyn put an apple and the cell phone in the saddle bag and tossed it over the golden back of the horse, just behind the saddle.

On impulse, she put in her camera. She was a rather good photographer and hoped to get better. She loved to take pictures and one never knew what they might see when riding out over the grassy mesa.

The sun shown warmly on her yellow hair and the breeze fanned against her face, waking her up from the boring bout with Beginning Algebra.

The tall grass reached as high as the belly of the pony. It was a mixture of yellow-green buffalo grass, and the gray-green stems of the prairie bluestem grass. Flat as a tabletop, the meadow spread all the way to the lip of the huge box canyon.

A small river flowed down from somewhere in the far off foothills and poured over the lip of the canyon in a silver spray of a waterfall that would be the envy of the wedding veil in any bridal shop.

The river water was made up mostly from snowmelt from the distant mountains and it flowed across the high meadow, cascading over the lip of the canyon, and falling with a roar into the rock-bottomed pool. From there it spilled over into a small lake.

When it flowed from the lake, it gathered itself back into being a river, and wound its way across the floor of the canyon. After that, it flowed away, maybe all the way to the Mississippi and into the Gulf of Mexico.

Caitlyn loved the box canyon. It was called a 'box' canyon because it was surrounded with walls like a huge bowl. It was located on land leased by the ranch for their horses and longhorns, but a lot of other animals claimed it as well. Wolves and foxes and smaller animals were often seen there, as well as bison, often called buffalo along with a herd of American elk, an animal that was originally called wapiti.

The only reason she was allowed to ride out alone was that she carried the cell phone and could always be located, and also could call for help if she should need it.

Across the familiar tall grass the golden pony trotted, joyful to escape the stable. Caitlyn bounced happily on her back, just as joyful to escape her lessons.

At the narrow trail that led down into the canyon, Golden slowed, picking her way on careful hooves. The steepness of the trail tried to pitch Caitlyn forward over the pony's head, but she had ridden this trail many times. She knew just how to hold on.

Finally on the canyon floor, the palomino lowered her head to grab a bite of the juicy grass, but Caitlyn reined her up. "You can eat later while I climb on the rock ledges."

The pony trotted around the wall of the canyon, stopping by the rock outcroppings where Caitlyn often brought her. She lowered her head and again began to graze, as she had been promised.

The girl leaped to the ground and ran to the rocks. It was such fun the way the flat stones jutted out from the wall of the bluff like the steps of a very wide ladder. She could climb from one to the other, though some of the steps were quite a long stretch for her legs.

Today, the stretching felt incredibly good.

High on her favorite ledge, she sat and swung her feet over the edge while she watched her grazing pony. Then she looked, with dismay, down at her feet. In her haste to be gone, she had not changed into her riding boots and here she was, climbing the rough rocks in light casual loafers.

Bad idea. The slickness of the soles made them a bit dangerous and she could get hurt. In addition, the climbing and scuffing was not doing the shoes any good either. Oh, well...

And it was at that moment that one of the loafers dropped off her foot. Oops! Toe over heel the shoe tumbled, kicking dust puffs here and there, and it came to rest on a small ledge much closer to the canyon floor than the ledge where she sat. Well, she'd get it when she came down, and now she would just have to be sock-footed on one foot. She'd also have to watch out for the cactus stickers in her sock.

Caitlyn climbed about on the rocks until the sun lowered to the canyon lip and that was her signal to head for home. Working her way down, she reached the place where her shoe waited.

The shoe was full of dust and gravel, so she whacked the heel against the rock ledge to knock out the dirt. It was then that a chunk of the clay between the rock ledges slid away, revealing something behind it.

She had been warned never to poke her hands into a strange place. Who knew what might be in there? So she used a stick to work the object out from under the rock ledge.

It seemed to be something wrapped in cloth and the old cotton fabric of the wrapping was very rotten. It broke into crumbles when it was touched.

An idea!

Jumping to the ground, she rooted around in the saddlebag for her camera. Aiming the camera high, she took a snapshot of the ledge containing the strange package, while standing on the ground, then climbed back up and took another picture. The hiding place was hardly more than eight feet above the canyon floor.

Now, to get it down without tearing it up!

Another good idea! She slipped off her shirt and then her undershirt. Putting her shirt back on, she carefully slid the crumbling package onto her undershirt. Gently folding the soft knit around it, she slid down the bank and put it on the ground. Then she climbed back up and got her shoe.

Crouching on the ground, she carefully peeled back the rotted fabric of the item and what she saw made thrill bumps raise up on her arms. A little shiver of suspense played along her shoulders and down her back.

Right there before her on the old cloth was a small book and a tiny rag doll, hardly longer than her hand. The old, stained cloth fabric of the doll's body was not much better than the wrapping, so she lifted the doll carefully with both hands and slipped it into the loafer beside her. So what if she rode home with one sock foot in the stirrup!

Carefully she put the shoe into the saddlebag so it would not tip over and spill the fragile toy. The small book was in somewhat better condition, though it was yellowed and crumbling. Beside the book was a stub of a pencil that appeared to have been sharpened with a knife.

Slipping the wooden pencil into her shirt pocket, she carefully opened the book. On the flyleaf was printed, This Book Belongs to, and then there was a line. Still readable was the name on the line, Annie Jo Cantrell.

The shiver of thrill bumps again raced down her back. A diary! It seemed this book must be the diary of a girl named Annie who, for some reason, had hidden her book in the rock ledges of a box canyon on the tall grass mesa of Oklahoma.

This was clearly the beginning of a mystery, and no one loved mysteries more than Caitlyn.

Carefully she lifted the flyleaf of the small book and a chunk of the yellowed paper broke off in her fingers.

- END OF EXCERPT -

ADDITIONAL BOOK SERIES
BY JOANN KLUSMEYER

The Great I Am Bible Story Series for Kids
6 books

The Young Pioneers Adventure Series for Kids
5 books

The Wentworth Triplets Mystery Series for Young Teens
3 books

Footsteps in the Canyon Adventure Series for Young Teens
4 books

Burnt Tree Junction Historical Fiction Series for Adults
6 books

Ozark Mountains Historical Fiction Series for Adults
7 books

Taming the Wilderness Historical Fiction Series for Adults
4 books

The Sheltering Stones Historical Fiction Series for Adults
5 books

The Trilogy of Wishbone Hollow Historicial Fiction Series for Adults
3 books

www.ingramcontent.com/pod-product-compliance
Lightning Source LLC
Chambersburg PA
CBHW060839250626

47162CB00005B/2112